GOLD HOCKEY SERIES

GOLD CAST OF CHARACTERS

Heroes and Heroines:

Brit Plantain (Blocked) — first female goalie in the NHL, loves boy bands

Stefan Barie (Blocked) — captain of the Gold

Sara Jetty (Backhand) — artist and figure skater

Mike Stewart (Backhand) —defenseman for the Gold, romance guru

Blane Hart (Boarding) — center for the Gold, number 22

Mandy Shallows (Boarding) — trainer and physical therapist

Max Montgomery (Benched) — defensemen for the Gold, giant nerd

Angelica Shallows (Benched) — engineer at RoboTech, also a giant nerd

Blue Anderson (Breakaway) — top forward in the league and for the Gold

Anna Hayes (Breakaway) — Max's former nanny, no relation to Kevin Hayes

Rebecca Stravokraus (Breakout) — Gold publicist, makes killer brownies, known at PR-Rebecca

Kevin Hayes (Breakout) — forward for the Gold, no relation to Anna Hayes

Changed

Gold Hockey #19

Elise Faber

CHANGED
BY ELISE FABER
Newsletter sign-up

This is a work of fiction. Names, places, characters, and events are fictitious in
every regard. Any similarities to actual events and persons, living or dead, are
purely coincidental. Any trademarks, service marks, product names, or named
features are assumed to be the property of their respective owners, and are used
only for reference. There is no implied endorsement if any of these terms are used.
Except for review purposes, the reproduction of this book in whole or part,
electronically or mechanically, constitutes a copyright violation.

Rebecca Hallbright (Checked) — nutritionist for the Gold, plethora of delicious vegan recipes, known as Nutrionist-Rebecca

Gabe Carter (Checked) — doctor, head trainer for the Gold

Calle Stevens (Coasting) — assistant coach for the Gold, former national team member

Coop Armstrong (Coasting) — talented forward on the Gold, addicted to historical romance audiobooks

Mia Caldwell (Centered) — 5th degree black belt, brings the snark

Liam Williamson (Centered) — Gold forward finding his love for the game, charming and pushy in equal measures

Charlotte Harris (Charging) — new Gold GM, hates losing and the game Chubby Bunny

Logan Walker (Charging) — defensemen for the Gold, skills include: cockiness and being able to buy presents that make Charlotte squirm

Dani Eastbrook (Caged) — video coach for the Gold, tech nerd, could fix your computer in a flash, shy

Ethan Korhonen (Caged) — forward for the Gold, killer power play skills, known as Big Juicy Brain

Fanny Douglas (Crashed) — silver medalist, skating coach for the Gold

Brandon Cunningham (Crashed) — brown curls, penchant for hallways, Kaydon Lewis's agent

Kaydon Lewis (Cycled)— yummy stubble, great with kids, doesn't mind a little snot

Scarlett Andrews (Cycled)—quiet, perfectionist, resembled Bambi on ice

Charlie Andrews (Caught)— Scarlett's brother and total romantic

Kacee (Caught)— the woman inside the giant Gold nugget

Joshua Webb (Cap)— tall, smart, and handsome, the newest captain of the Gold

Jess White (Cap)— assistant video coach and obsessed with a certain new captain

Benjamin Roberts (Covered)— snarky, smart, and dipping a toe where he shouldn't

Jordyn Webb (Covered)— single mom and Josh's sister

Will Johansson (Crushed)— smart, sensitive, and likes Shirley Temples

Lily Cartwright (Crushed)— sports psychologist and obsessed with fluffy pancakes

Additional Characters:

Bernard — head coach

Richie — equipment manager

Dan Plantain — Brit's brother

Diane Barie — Stefan's mom

Pierre Barie — Stefan's dad, owner of the Gold

Spence — former goalie, married to Monique, daughter Mirabel

Monique — married to Spence, former model

Mirabel — daughter of Spence and Monique

Mitch — Sara's boss

Allison and Sean — Blane's parents

Pascal — Devon Scott's security lead

Roger Shallows — Mandy's dad

Grant and Megan — Devon's parents

ONE

MADS

S he sighed as she pulled her key from the lock and checked that the door was secure.

Exhaustion filled every single one of her cells, swelling them until they threatened to burst.

Or maybe that was just her head.

Because...the noise.

Good God, the noise tonight had been...

Ear-piercing.

The center's first movie night had been a huge success. They'd been at max capacity, and everyone had behaved, chowing on popcorn and junk food and watching the first in a trilogy of superhero movies.

Everyone had gotten along.

Smiles had abounded.

And she'd been asked no less than a dozen times when the next movie night would be.

So...success.

But God, her ears were still ringing.

Her nephews were loud, but they had nothing on a collective of teenagers hopped up on sugar and fraternizing with their peers.

Still, it felt good.

Not in the blissful numbness that had once been her obsession—seeking, desperate for it, her entire existence reduced to searching for it. Rather, in a tired and fulfilled and proud of something she was doing for once in her life.

Living in the here and now.

In the pain of a sore body and pounding head and tired mind.

And...being okay with that. Not trying to numb it.

Knowing that she'd be okay with a Tylenol.

Knowing that she could sit in her mind and body and *be* okay.

"You're fine," she whispered, turning for the parking lot and her junker. She'd almost saved enough to buy a new—or at least a new to her—car.

Maybe she'd get one with automatic locks.

Smiling to herself, she absently rubbed her head as she walked to her car, dug out her keys, and unlocked the driver's side door.

She pulled at the handle, bent to slide in—

Which was the exact moment that hell broke loose.

A hand landed on her shoulder, and it wasn't heavy, wasn't hard, the grip wasn't painful...but her mind didn't care, her body —remembering all the things she tried to keep buried—just... reacted.

"Don't fucking touch me!" she screamed, twisting away, fear making her movements sharp and jerky and strong.

The hand disappeared.

"Shit, I'm—"

But the door didn't.

It was right where she'd left it—the heavy steel panel half open. And with her sharp and jerky and strong movements, it was right there in her face.

Colliding with her face.

She cried out as pain exploded from her temple, along her jaw, something wet and hot dripping down her face. *Blood* dripping down her face. Her knees hit the pavement, the pain over-whelming her for a moment before she remembered herself, remembered that it was dark and she was alone in the parking lot—

Not alone.

Someone had grabbed her.

She clawed at the doorframe and managed to get to her feet, vision blurry as she scrabbled to pull herself into the front seat.

"Shit, Mads."

That voice.

It penetrated the haze of pain and both soothed the panic inside her and increased it until it swelled up her throat, made it nearly impossible for her to breathe in anything other than short gasps of air. She'd gone still. Frozen. Hell, she couldn't move.

He could not be here.

He could not see her like this.

Not her in pieces and hurting and scared.

Not her bleeding and pathetic and—

That hand came to her face and, this time, the touch was tentative as Lucas lightly gripped her chin and turned her head toward him.

Another curse, his thumb gently running along her jaw.

"I'm so sorry, honey," he murmured.

Then he let her go.

Leaving her alone and bleeding in the driver's seat of her car.

It wasn't the first time she'd found herself in the same situation. She'd deal. She always did.

Wincing, she reached for the keys from where they'd dropped onto the pavement when Lucas had startled her and rotated care-fully so that she could insert them into the ignition. Her car rumbled to life. A reach had her head throbbing, but she managed to get her glove box open to extract a stack of napkins, which she pressed to her temple, used to wipe the blood from her jaw.

Good enough.

It hurt, but it didn't seem like it was actively dripping any longer.

Go platelets.

She tossed the napkins onto the passenger's seat, sat down, and moved to yank her door closed—

A hand caught it.

Her heart skipped a beat, but then Lucas's face appeared in the opening.

He tugged it wider, squatted in the opening. "Let me help you, Peaches," he said, holding up a first aid kit.

She blinked.

Then again when he didn't disappear, when it became suspect that she wasn't actually confused, that this was really happening —the man who hated her viscerally was offering to help her—

She, uh...she didn't react well.

Or, rather, she reacted in typical Mads fashion.

Imprudently.

She jerked her head back, shoving Lucas away from her as she slammed the door shut. A heartbeat later, she threw her car into drive and screeched out of the parking lot.

Leaving Lucas standing next to where she'd been parked, holding that first aid kit.

As she drove off.

Alone.

Because that was what she deserved.

Two

LUCAS

He was an idiot thinking that she would show up here, that the first aid kit he'd retrieved from his trunk, the one that was sitting on his passenger's seat right at that very moment would be put to good use.

Because she would come here.

What did he know about Mads Roberts?

Nothing.

Only that he knew her sort.

But he'd been to Mafia's with her more times than he'd been happy about in the last year-plus, ever since she and Ben had made up and started to begin rebuilding their relationship.

Ever since his protective instincts had been pricked.

For his friend.

Not for Mads.

Because...circling back to knowing her sort.

Intimately. Living with them, trying to break free from their clinging tentacles, to unhook their sharp, deeply embedded hooks.

He didn't want that for Ben.

Didn't want that for his friend.

Mads might have fooled everyone with her whole turned-over-a-new-leaf bullshit, but he didn't buy it, not for a fucking second. Sooner or later, those claws would come out and they would sink deep into Ben's skin, deep enough to scour his heart, his soul.

And since Ben didn't see that, it was Lucas's job to protect.

His friend.

Not Mads.

Though, he could have done without the side of her attempting to brain herself on the car door, something that was his fucking fault and why he was sitting here at Mafia's—hoping that for once in his life she *would* show up—in the first place, two burgers on the way and a beer in front of him.

Watching the door.

Waiting to see if the bell would jingle softly and Mads would walk through the door and—

"Hey, big guy," a sultry voice murmured, followed very closely by a hand settling on his shoulder, trailing down his arm.

Much like he'd been attempting to do to Mads.

Catching her attention.

Finally doing what he should have—warning her away from Ben, from his friend and his family that was the Gold.

Might the impetus to impart that hard truth have come from a phone call just before he drove by the youth center and saw Mads walking to her car?

Maybe.

But it was something he'd put off doing for far too long anyway.

He should have drawn the boundary before, should have—

Those fingers tightened on his forearm, and he blinked...and if it was blinking away the image of Mads hitting the door, the blood on her face, the bruise already blooming on her temple, forcing away the sound of her head colliding with the metal, her pained cry that had followed was hard as fuck then that was just because—

Well, just *because*.

It didn't matter anyway because he *did* push it away, he *did* manage to focus on the present...

And on the gorgeous blonde currently sidling up next to him.

Was she a little plastic?

Yeah, but he didn't mind that. A girl wanted to wear makeup and get Botox or paint her skin like a clown and somehow have that turn into a gorgeous face like in all those TikTok videos? Go for it. She wanted to wear nothing but sunscreen and live in T-shirts and sweats? Awesome. He liked a woman who was comfortable in her own skin, who lived how she wanted to, no matter what she looked like.

So why did dark brown curls and olive skin and lush pink lips come to mind when his gaze traced along the blonde's body?

Fit, tits that could be fake but bounced like they were real when she leaned in, that flawless face on display, her voice like sin when she invited him back to her place.

No preamble.

Comfortable with herself.

Confident in asking for what she wanted.

So why did he picture a woman who had a thread of vulnerable laced through each and every movement, who spent her life with her shoulders hunched, seeming to want to blend into the background?

It was a trap, a façade that she held on to—

Only, *was* it?

"So, what do you say, big guy?" came that sultry voice again, her hand having moved beyond his forearm, down to his knee, and was now working itself way up his thigh.

Closing in on the motherland.

Only...his dick didn't so much as twitch, even as her fingers brushed along the length of him.

Even when that brush became more than a brush.

"Want to come home with me?" she asked, wrapping her

hand around his cock—or as much as she was able with him wearing jeans.

And still his dick didn't react, just lay limp against his thigh.

But he was opening his mouth to say yes because that was what he always did.

The offer was there. He was single.

Why not make a fun night out of it?

It was just...the fun nights had been coming less and less frequently. Mostly because—

"Here you go."

He glanced up, saw that the server had returned, this time with two plates of steaming hot burgers—barbecue bacon and cheddar with fries for him, onion rings for the not yet arrived Mads. "Thanks," he murmured, dislodging the blonde enough to take the plate that the waiter, Tom, held out.

Tom winked and set the other plate down in front of Propositioning McGee. "Will your date need anything else?"

The blonde froze, looked to the plate full of greasy goodness and wrinkled her nose.

Right.

That's why his dick wasn't working.

He couldn't be with someone who didn't cut loose when it came to food. Life was too fucking short to not enjoy a meal that provided absolutely no nutritional value and he spent too much damned time following a restrictive meal plan that, while it worked, was still restrictive.

He was breaking with convention by ordering a burger on a non-Cheat Day.

But...he'd thought, or maybe hoped, that she would show up.

"No," octopus woman sneered at Tom. Something that had me immediately nudging her back. "I don't *want* anything."

Only the rest of her sentence was nonverbal.

I don't want anything...from you.

But from the hockey player who has a big paycheck and a bigger cock—

Right. He couldn't be with someone who talked to people like that, who used a tone like *that* with people who were just living their life, just trying to get their shit done.

You've used that same tone plenty with Mads, asshole.

That was different.

Mads was—

"You sure?" Tom asked, only this time it wasn't directed at the woman, but rather at Lucas.

Still paired with another nonverbal statement, though. As in, *What the fuck? Are you serious with this chick?*

He wasn't serious.

He didn't even know her name.

Which was why he nudged her again, this time so she was out of the booth. "It's not happening tonight."

Her face changed, the hard edges that had appeared with Tom's and the burgers' arrival softening, her plump bottom lip coming out, expression becoming pleading.

"Nice try," Lucas said. "But I can see through that face." He jerked his chin back toward the bar, where a gaggle of similar plastic-like women sat tittering on barstools. "Move along, honey."

For a second, it seemed as though she would protest, but he just lifted his brows, waited her out.

A huff as she turned and flounced away.

"Thanks for the assist," he told Tom once she was far enough away.

A shrug. "Figured it'd work. That one looked like she wouldn't eat so much as a salad in front of a man."

Lucas snorted. "Yeah, I could see that."

"You meeting one of the guys?" Tom asked, eyes flicking to the second plate then coming back to Lucas's.

He *could* tell the truth about who the second burger was for.

He chose to lie.

"Yeah, but the fucker canceled on me," he said. "Could you wrap that up for me?" Shifting to the side, he freed his wallet from his back pocket, pulled out some cash. "And close me out?"

Tom glanced at the bar, probably tagging the same truth that Lucas had.

The blonde was planning her alternate attack.

"On it," Tom said, taking the cash and plate and bustling away, returning a few minutes later with a boxed-up burger and Lucas's change—even though Lucas had told the server a dozen times to *always* keep the change.

Lucas passed it back, downed his burger, his beer.

Then he went home.

And ate the second lukewarm one as punishment.

Thank God no one was there to call him on the fact it wasn't a Cheat Day.

THREE

MADS

"Aunt Mads!"

She jerked, having just let herself through the side gate, bracing for the likely chance that Lucas would be at the team get-together at her brother's house. But with all that bracing, she wasn't paying attention, so she nearly dropped the bags she was lugging in.

Of course, her nephews were putting their eagle eyes to good use.

She'd been flakey lately, avoiding exactly this type of event.

After that night at the youth center, after Lucas had seen her bloody and freaked, she'd...been avoiding.

Running, hiding, and doing it long enough that Ben was worried.

Which hurt, even as she understood why.

Running, hiding, *avoiding*—all hallmarks of her personality when she was using. Along with bitchy, selfish, and really fucking *mean*.

Some might even say more than a little evil.

All in all, a total catch.

Who wouldn't want to spend time with her?

"Aunt Mads!" Samuel cried again, only this time from closer and approximately zero-point-two seconds before Sam's little—or not *so* little anymore, since he was growing like a weed—body slammed into hers, nearly upending the bags a second time. "You're here!"

Another reason she had bitten the bullet and promised to come tonight.

Her nephews—technically step-nephews, but they were part of Ben's life and heart, so part of hers as well—had missed her. She'd heard the disappointment in their voices the last time she put off a visit, their sadness slicing through her, even though she'd just been talking to Ben on FaceTime and they'd been goofing around in the background. Already feeling guilty for worrying her brother, she couldn't take the combined guilt of her nephews too.

Hence, being here for the barbecue.

"I *am* here," she said, hugging him back as well as she could with the bags hanging from her wrists. "And I've brought you something."

He jumped back, excitement on his adorable little boy face. "What is it?" he asked, bouncing a little on the balls of his feet.

Cute.

She lifted her arm, wiggling her hand so the bag would slide off her wrist and passed it over to him. "Is your brother aro—"

"Aunt Mads!"

Heavier footsteps coming her way, a body hitting hers, albeit without the side of heavy collision his brother had wrought, and Marcus was hugging her tight.

"Hey, sweetie," she said, lifting one loaded-down arm with a herculean effort and reaching into the tote hanging at her elbow. "Here." She tugged out the book she'd found for him. "I think it's the one—"

Those arms closed around her again, tight enough to send the air shooting from her lungs in a *whoosh*. "Thank you, Aunt

Mads," Marcus said quietly. "I've been wanting to read this forever."

Not because Ben or their mom, Jordyn, didn't buy the boys books, but because Marcus's to-be-read list was about a mile long, and considering that her own TBR was in similar shape, she had no problem chipping in and feeding his reading addiction.

"Whoa!"

Marcus released her, and she glanced over at Sammy—or *Sam* as she was trying to remember to call him since he was now "grown up" and preferred it. For all that growing up, he was wearing a little boy's excitement (because he was still a little boy) as he *oohed* and *aahed* over the Lego set she'd found for him.

Nothing crazy like the huge sets her brother built with him.

But it was Star Wars themed and she hadn't seen it before.

"If you already have it," she began, "I have the receipt and you can—"

A whirl, his body slamming into hers again. "Thank you, Aunt Mads," he said. "It's awesome! Want to build it with me?"

Her heart convulsed.

This was why she'd gotten her shit together, why she kept it together.

Kids like Marcus and Sammy—*Sam*—who'd had it tough, who had trauma and baggage and deserved to have lightness in their hearts, even if it was just for a moment. Not focusing on their asshole of a dad who'd cheated and left them. Not focusing on what they'd missed out on.

Living their lives big and bright *now*.

Despite the past.

She hadn't done that, hadn't the strength or the safe space, especially after her brother had moved out.

Now she wanted to make sure other kids had the chance to do things differently.

It was why she worked at the youth center.

Trying to encourage them to not focus on their parents who were neglectful or addicts who made their lives so fucking difficult. Trying to get them to seek out help for their own addictions they'd fallen into because drugs or alcohol were forced on them. Or the drugs and booze were just there and available and a path to escape and now they couldn't stop.

Whatever the reason they'd come in her circle, her ultimate goal was to give them a safe place. Even if it was just in the evenings and on the weekends, the center was somewhere they could eat something, learn safely, participate in activities like art and music or just watching a movie they wouldn't be able to afford to see otherwise.

There were counselors and a garden, classrooms and volunteers who ran enrichment programs. And there are people like her brother and the other guys from the Gold who came in to inspire and take their minds off the shit in her kids' lives.

And raise money.

So they could have those programs.

But more importantly, she was committed to making sure her kids had that safe place.

It was why her couch had been used by some of the kids more than once.

Why her gaze scanned the road on her drive home, always looking out for a familiar figure who might need help.

Why she would never let herself slip.

They needed her to be stable and available and there for them, even if they didn't always trust her or her staying power.

Eventually, they came around.

Because she knew about difficult childhoods and people who tried to make lives harder.

No. Scratch that.

She knew about people who were evil and took advantage of a young girl at rock bottom.

And she knew about being an addict.

Thankfully, she'd found somewhere she could make a difference and have a purpose that wasn't her and the demons that liked to claw at her brain.

"How about we build it after the party?" she said to Sam, forcing the past away and focusing on her nephews. "That way I can catch up with the adults and you can play with the kids while it's still light out."

He paused, head tilting as he considered that. "Okay!" One more squeeze before he released her and raced off.

Marcus was already flipping through his new book and she managed to get another bag off her wrist. "And here's the rest of the series," she whispered, passing him the tote.

His eyes went wide. "Really?"

"Really," she said, mouth curving as he took it and immediately went in search of a quiet corner, steps slow as he began devouring the pages.

The books were the least he deserved.

The least she could do.

Plus, he'd probably finish book one that night and it was awful having to wait for the next one. This way he could plow through the entire series, one after another and not have to—

"You don't have to do that, you know."

Mads turned, saw that Jordyn had come up to her, beautiful as always and doubly so with the slight baby bump that was highlighted in her softly patterned blouse. Jordyn and her brother would be cutting it close with the baby's arrival and the post-season (especially if the Gold went all the way). Something Mads knew since the pregnancy wasn't entirely planned. But her brother and Jordyn were still thrilled to have another kiddo on the way to join their family.

Try as everyone might to plan ahead, sometimes fate had a hand in life.

And in babies.

Her womb ached, where she'd once carried her own baby, but she pushed that away. She didn't push it away like she used to, though, didn't shove it down into a deep dark corner of her soul and slam the lid shut, throwing on a padlock and chain, burying it in dirt. She didn't push it away and pretend it didn't exist.

She let the pain and grief wash over her.

Then she allowed it to slide away, to dull.

Not hiding. Not numb. Living life with all its joys and hurts.

"Have you told the boys?" she asked softly, instead of acknowledging Jordyn's soft admonishment for bringing goodies for the boys.

First, Mads had a lot to make up for.

Second, the boys were sweet, humble, and never ungrateful.

Third, they deserved the world.

Fourth, she'd do it for their smiles alone.

Fifth—

Well, Jordyn saved her from her mental list of reasons she could spoil her nephews (hint: they were infinite). "Yes," she said, smoothing a hand over her belly. Her mouth curved. "They've demanded a baby sister."

Mads's baby had been a little girl.

Another pulse of pain rolling over her skin, another slice to push away.

She exhaled silently, accepted the hurts, and...let them go. "They'd be great with a sister." She smiled at her sister-in-law. "Or a brother."

Jordyn's own smile was serene. "I know." It went a little chagrined. "Though I can't say that I'm sad about the possibility of having to buy little girl clothes."

Ruffles and polka dots.

Hair bows and matching diaper covers.

Plus all the normal baby adorableness.

She *couldn't* wait to spoil her new niece or nephew—but hopefully niece, if solely for the shopping fun that would come her way. "I know," she said. "I've—"

"Aunt Mads!"

She turned to see Marcus and Sammy—*Sam*—both running her way.

"Uh-oh," Jordyn said. "If you want adult interaction, now's the moment to run before they dominate your social time."

Social time with hockey players.

Who were cool but knew she'd hurt her brother, their teammate.

Well, potentially spending time with one who *wasn't* cool because he knew she'd hurt his teammate.

One who'd seen her make a fool out of herself—panicking and bonking her head and bleeding all over her shirt.

One who'd—

No, who *was* walking into the back yard, a twelve-pack of beer in his hand.

She jerked her gaze away, tossed a smile that was probably fake as hell at Jordyn. "I'll just go and see what the boys need."

Because having her social time with her two nephews who adored her, even despite her flaws, sounded fucking great.

A hell of a lot better than being eviscerated by a man who might be beautiful.

But who hurt her soul.

FOUR

LUCAS

He was reclining on one of the chairs, sipping a beer.

And watching a certain brown-haired beauty.

Who seemingly never ran out of energy as she played a complicated game of tag with the kids, one he didn't understand—only that it seemed to have way too many rules.

What was wrong with just running and tagging someone?

They were crawling through legs and passing balls and tapping fists and—

No matter what new rule they added, she never grew tired or short with her tone.

It was...unfathomable.

Or maybe admirable.

Or maybe—

He shook himself.

It didn't matter.

Neither did the fact that she still had a hint of a bruise on her temple, something only he seemed to notice. Probably because he was the cause of it, knew where it was, mostly obfuscated by the makeup she'd obviously carefully applied.

But he saw it.

And felt the slice of guilt.

Not just for the injury—though that was deep and intense. For...starting to think that maybe he had misjudged her.

One barbecue and a couple of days volunteering did not make a good person.

But did months and months of trying to be one make—

"I'm back, bitch—er—" A glance around the yard, as Brit was mid-call, pausing and censoring herself. "—*boys*!" She strolled onto the deck with Roxie on her hip and Stefan at her shoulder.

"And girls!" Madeline—one of the Gold kids, this one belonging to the not-so-long-retired Blane and his wife and head trainer, Mandy.

"And girls," Brit agreed with a nod, putting a squirming Roxie down so she could go join the gaggle of kids.

"Girls!" Roxie yelled in her adorable toddler voice, little legs moving like The Flash.

Blane moved to Brit, kissing her cheek before sweeping her up into a giant bear hug. "Just couldn't stay away, could you?" he teased.

She punched him lightly on the shoulder when he settled her back onto her feet. "Like you have a leg to stand on, Mr. Already at the Team Barbecue."

A smirk. "Guilty." A beat. "Though, in fairness to me, my spouse still works with these jokers."

"Rude!" Ben called, tossing a beer to Brit and a mock glare to Blane. "There's the gate, feel free to see yourself out."

Josh grinned, slung an arm around Brit's shoulder and pulled their former goalie in for a hug. "Good to see you," he told Brit before glancing up at Blane. "You can go," he teased, "but we're keeping your wife."

Mandy laughed, holding their youngest in her arms. "I hate to be the bearer of bad news," she said, passing the baby over to Brit who began loving on her and earning baby giggles in return, "but I kind of like my hockey player." Mandy adjusted the baby's onesie, a sweet smile on her face. "So if you keep me, you've gotta keep him."

Hisses and boos abounded, but they were good natured and pretty soon Blane was settled in Lucas's chair while Lucas prepped a bottle.

It was impossible to not be comfortable with kids when it came to this crew.

He could change a diaper, prep a bottle. He knew that those fold things in the shoulders of a onesie gave enough space so it could be removed down instead of up. Hell, he knew that a onesie was called a onesie in the first place.

Kids didn't scare him.

He might even want some in a few years.

What *did* scare him was—

The baby squawked and Lucas snapped out of it, passing the bottle over. "How'd you talk Mandy into another kid?"

She'd sworn to be done.

Meanwhile...the baby in Blane's arms.

Blane who was smirking. "Do I need to give you the birds and the bees talk, Luc?"

Oh God, here they went.

"Never mind," he muttered, moving away from Blane and the baby, from the sight that made something yearn inside him, from his teammates who would heap on shit—shit he could normally laugh off, didn't mind being on the receiving end of, considering that he gave out plenty of crap in his own right. But that night, he wasn't in the mood.

And part of it was because of the woman running on the grass, spinning in circles and giggling like a loon with the kids, all of whom were equally as goofy.

Good with kids.

He wanted it to be bullshit, to be something he could poke at, find a flaw in.

But the more he watched, the less he found wrong.

And the more he watched her, the harder it was to look away.

Especially, when he watched her in a way that was neutral, his suspicion and prejudice set aside. He'd seen her playing with the kids—the only breaks she'd taken being when she'd stepped out of the game to build a Lego set with Sam, when she looked at the page in the book Marcus held out at her and they'd shared a pleased smile, when she got the kids a drink or snack or cleaned up a spill, kissed a boo-boo.

Why did the sight of Mads hugging a kid close, pressing a kiss to the top of her head make his heart squeeze?

He didn't even like her.

Or maybe—

"You look confused."

It didn't surprise him that Brit had sniffed out the whirlwind in his mind. Their former goalie was really good at being too fucking nosy, and the fact that she'd retired and now didn't have hockey to keep her occupied meant that she had even more time on her hands.

More time to be nosey as fuck.

Christ.

"I'm just tired," he lied. "I hit the gym hard this morning." Well, *that* part wasn't a lie. He was working his ass off, getting ready for the season. While they were playing, it was more about maintaining strength and staying healthy. The off-season was for building new muscle mass, increasing power and explosiveness and staying power. Because eighty-two games over eight months took a toll on a body and that wasn't even including the post-season.

"Hmm," Brit murmured, surprising him by not pushing, by just reclining on the set of steps where he'd sat and done his watching, her elbows propped up behind her.

And not speaking.

That was key.

She *didn't* speak.

Maybe retirement was really taking it out of her.

He mirrored her movements, elbows behind him, though he

didn't allow his gaze to match Brit's, to go to the group of kids on the lawn, to Mads running around with them.

Silence settled between him and his former teammate.

Children's happy screams in the air. The purples and oranges and deep reds of the sunset overhead, the navy and black where the sky met the softly rolling hills broken up with the strands of lights strung across the back yard.

The moon, yellow and almost perfectly round.

The stars, just beginning to twinkle.

Jupiter's bright white shape hanging at the southern horizon.

City lights in the distance.

And the fog rolling in.

San Francisco.

The city that had become his home.

This team that had become his family.

Which was the moment Brit ran out of patience.

"You know—"

He snorted when she started up. Because...of course. And, anyway, what had he been thinking? She wasn't the type to start a nosy intervention and then just let it go. She was a professional athlete—or had been one anyway. They didn't just let things go. They gripped reality in their teeth and skated it into oblivion... and waited for the right moment to pounce.

"—it's okay to be confused."

He blinked, glanced over at her, that not being the beginning of the inquisition he'd expected. "Are you losing your touch or just on a fishing expedition?" he asked when she didn't go on.

Because that had been...positively uninspired.

She flashed him that smile of hers, the one that graced billboards and was the face of toothpaste commercials. "Neither," she said and he couldn't tell if she was lying. "I saw you sitting over here, brows furrowed, purposely keeping your distance from everyone." She tapped a finger with a short, rounded nail that had been painted a deep blue across her bottom lip. "One might say *brooding.*"

Fuck.

He didn't need her reading anything into this.

He didn't need—

"And your gaze drifting over to a certain brunette."

Fuck.

"So," she said, pushing up to her feet and wiping off the back of her pants, pausing to stare down at him with impenetrable brown eyes, "all I'm saying is that it's okay to be conflicted." She bounded down the short staircase, started toward the kids—which was a good thing because Roxie had just spilled her container of bubbles and appeared a heartbeat away from a meltdown.

"But—"

He tore his gaze from Roxie—okay from *Mads*—and glanced back at Brit.

"—if you hurt her," Brit said. "*Again,*" she added, her brows flicking up, dark chocolate eyes pinning him in place, telling him that she was aware of exactly which of his actions were making him feel *conflicted*.

"*I* will hurt you."

Brit dropped that bomb then turned back for the kids.

And he sat on those stairs and felt...

Conflicted.

FIVE

MADS

She had the familiar beginning of a headache, but it wasn't from noise.

Not this time.

It was from worry.

For Olivia.

The petite redhead with arms and legs that were somehow both model-like *and* seemed too long for her body was off.

Her easy smiles were gone.

The shadows beneath her pale blue eyes were growing darker each and every time Mads saw her...something that was happening less and less as time went by.

Something that was sending Mads's spidey senses tingling.

She'd lived like that.

Growing quiet, internalizing everything, drawing herself tighter and tighter into a proverbial ball, trying to make it so if she was just small enough that everyone would stop noticing.

That *he* would stop noticing.

It hadn't worked.

And it wasn't going to work now—not because Mads was

going to hurt Olivia—she would *never* do that—but because Mads wasn't going to allow Olivia to slip through the cracks.

She *wasn't*.

But when she watched Olivia walk across the parking lot after shaking her head to Mads's offer to grab a bite to eat, her hands shoved into the pocket of her hoodie, head down and shoulders hunched, Mads worried that she wouldn't be able to stop it from happening.

Sighing—and vowing to not stop trying—she tugged the door to the center back open, moved down the hall and into the shoebox-sized office that was hers and hers alone. And, no lie, every time she saw her name on the plaque outside the door, her pulse picked up, her stomach fluttered, and...

It was hers.

She'd gone from crashing on couches (or on street corners when she was seriously fucked up or in a stranger's bed) to having an apartment and a car and her own office.

That she paid for herself.

Yeah, her brother'd had to co-sign with her because her credit was shit and it would take time for it to recover. Yeah, he'd put the security deposit down and filled her apartment with furniture—something she'd protested strongly.

But he was Ben.

And when he got something in his mind, he wasn't easy to convince otherwise.

Even *if* a certain teammate of his had given her brother a look, one that seemed to say, *Don't burn through your money on someone who doesn't deserve it.*

Lucas was there on move-in day—most of the Gold were—and she'd seen the look.

Seen the way *he'd* looked at *her* afterward.

The disgust...and the warning.

To not fuck with his friend.

Mads loved her brother, and she'd already done far too much

to hurt him. She sure as shit didn't have any plans to hurt him again, visual threat from Lucas or not.

Exhaling, she pushed the annoying hockey player from her head and rubbed the beginning of that throb in her temple as she sat down at her computer, focusing on what she needed to do to get out of there and home to her comfortable apartment. Step one, Georgia's house and the work there. Step two, home. Step three, bra off. Step four—this was the final step before she passed out—was a long, hot bath, so hot that she was at risk of scalding, that it would leave her skin flushed and bright pink.

Wash away the day.

Wash away the past.

But first...paperwork and emails and planning for the next couple of weeks.

A sip of water and then she was focusing, fingers flying on the keyboard, filing the necessary reports, balancing her budget spreadsheet, and then the fun part—planning.

She'd been given Mia's—one of the Gold WAGs (WAGs which, for those out of the loop—like herself—meant wives and girlfriends of the guys on the team)—phone number. Mia was a total BAMF (also an acronym she'd just learned because she wasn't hip or cool—badass motherfucker) and married to Liam. Mia also ran a karate studio, had a black belt, and had offered to come by the youth center to teach the kids some self-defense.

For free.

Which fit into Mads's budget perfectly.

Even with the Gold picking up the center as one of their patronages, they still ran on a shoestring budget that she stretched almost to breaking point.

So, free was great.

It was perfect.

She made the call, sent over the necessary paperwork (more paperwork, she knew) that Mia needed to complete to volunteer and since Mia was on top of things, Mads knew it would be sooner rather than later the badass black belt goddess was going to be helping her kids protect themselves.

Mads repeated, it was perfect.

By the time she'd hung up, it was cutting it close to getting over to Georgia's, so she hustled through the rest of the necessary tasks and saved everything that would hold to complete the next day.

Then she was hurrying out of her office, out of the youth center, making sure that the alarm was activated and the door had locked behind her. And shivering immediately because night had fallen while she was working and she might be in California, but that coastal wind could be a real bitch, especially when her jacket was in the trunk of her car.

Ah, fall.

Cold in the morning.

Hot enough midday that she peeled off her layers when she ate lunch (and stored them in the aforementioned trunk).

Frosty by nightfall.

She beelined for her car, not paying attention to the parking lot, or the fact that it was mostly empty. She'd been in far worse situations, and she couldn't live her life jumping at shadows—

"Or at touch," she whispered, her temple pulsing in pain, giving her an unwanted reminder of the other night with Lucas. "You have to get over it." A sigh as she popped the trunk. "You have to get over *all* of it."

She needed to pretend it hadn't happened with Lucas, ignore the disdain.

She needed to keep moving forward and living the small, bright life she was building where she actually was able to help other people and put the selfishness of her addiction behind her.

She *needed* to remember that her past self wasn't her.

That was the hardest one.

The barbed truth that struck at her on quiet evenings just like this.

She'd been hurt, yes, but she was also responsible for her own behavior and—

Her eyes stung, throat closing up, images threatening to close in on her.

But...she pushed it down.

She was *really* good at that.

Then, vision blurry, she dug around in the back of her trunk, struggling to find her jacket through the watery lenses. But managing because she was good at that. Good at persevering. Good at getting through.

"Exactly," she whispered to herself, tugging on the Gold-emblazoned fleece she'd stolen from her brother.

One of the few things she *didn't* regret stealing.

Namely because he'd grinned at her when she'd teased him about taking the borrowed jacket home, and that grin had belonged to her *brother*.

The Ben of old.

Not the one she'd hurt, who was filled with regret.

Just...*her* Ben.

And now every time she wore it around him, he tugged at a lock of her hair and shook his head, calling her "Maddy Girl."

She'd always loved that nickname.

Always loved the way his voice and face went soft when he called her that.

So yeah, no regrets about stealing the jacket.

And no regrets about it warming her right then, engulfing her in fabric from shoulders to knees, especially on this cold night.

She *did* have regrets about plenty of other things.

So many other things.

Which was why she got into her car, and instead of driving home and taking her bra off and getting into that scalding hot tub, she did her Step One.

She drove to Georgia's.

Six

LUCAS

He didn't know why he was at the youth center, why he'd spent hours sitting in the dark, in his cold-ass car. He didn't know why he couldn't get Mads out of his head.

Why his gaze was glued to her as she came out of the center, as she fussed with the door, and dug around in her trunk.

He didn't know why he followed her when she got in her car and turned left.

Instead of right.

Her apartment was to the right.

That was what piqued his senses.

The *only* thing he told himself.

She was supposed to be going to the right, supposed to be going home after work—

God, he sounded like an asshole.

There might be any number of things she would be doing after working all day. Grocery shopping, going to a meeting, getting a bite to eat at Mafia's—

Why did his heart skip a beat at that thought?

Because he might run into her or—

"No," he muttered. Not that. And anyway, she'd just missed the turn to head to the burger restaurant. His stomach grumbled in protest, but it wasn't a Cheat Day, so he couldn't eat there anyway. He was on for tofu and greens, beans, and plant protein that night. And chocolate cottage cheese ice cream for dessert.

All of which...sounded much less appetizing than a burger, fries, and a shake.

But all of which wasn't too bad. It was actually quite tasty and fulfilling and it helped him play hockey, so he couldn't complain.

Hockey that was starting soon.

He would be getting on the ice for the first of many team practices the following week, and he'd played today—well, he'd fucked around with Brit and Rome and a few of the other guys, teasing Brit about her "old lady retired status" while getting his feet under him and his hands back into action.

He hadn't spent a lot of time on the ice over the summer. It was mostly training and building muscle, hitting the gym and lifting weights and using the resistance band so often his muscles ached in protest if he even saw one at this point. Of course, this had all been after taking a full week off. Sitting on a beach. Not worrying about diets and plant-based grains and macronutrients. Just sitting on that stretch of shore, his toes shoved into the sand, the sun overhead, the waves crashing in the distance, and a book open on his lap.

No hockey. No team obligations. No hard workouts.

No teammates to worry about. No family to dig their claws in. No Mads to do the same to his friend.

That week had been the only true break he'd allowed himself.

Then it had been back to San Francisco, back to the gym, back to the team that was his family—way more than his biological one had ever been.

Getting strong. Getting ready. Getting—

"What the fuck?" he whispered as he watched Mads's car turn down a dark street...one that led into a really shitty neighborhood.

One that was full of gang members and drug busts and—

He fucking *knew* it.

Growling, he took the corner probably a little too fast, but his watching and not driving meant that he was losing sight of Mads's car as the rust bucket rumbled down the street. She pulled to a stop in front of a small light-colored house. It was gray or white or light brown or blue, but it was too dark—and the streetlights overhead were out—for him to see the exact shade. And anyway, he was less focused on the color and more on the fact that Mads was getting out of her car, her gaze darting around the street, her hands gripping the strap of her purse as she dashed up the cracked concrete pathway and knocked at the door.

Gaze still swiveling, shoulders still hunched.

Like she was uncomfortable.

Like she knew she was doing something wrong.

After a long moment—fuckers inside were probably seeing what kind of fucked-up person was on their porch—the door cracked open and Mads greeted whoever was on the other side.

Words were exchanged for several long moments.

Then the door swung wider and Mads disappeared inside the dark, broken-down house.

In the neighborhood known for drug deals.

He'd known she was hiding who she truly was from everyone.

He had fucking *known* it.

Seven

MADS

"Next time don't worry about cleaning the fans, honey," Georgia said softly, wincing when she lifted the ice pack and paper towel off Mads's arm.

An angry red cut sat below it, marring her skin and making her feel more than a little lightheaded.

Give her the prize for being the drug addict who was bad with blood.

Queasy always.

Dizzy always.

Luckily, it never lasted long, as though her instincts took over and reminded her that a little blood was nothing to worry about.

Making it stop so she could get away was more important.

"It's not the fan," she said, taking the paper towel back so she could cover the cut up, putting pressure on the area so the bleeding would stop and she felt well enough to drive home. "It's just me. I'm a klutz."

Georgia tsked and shook her head. "I shouldn't have had that statue there."

The broken statue, the shards of which now sat in a pile on the dustpan, Georgia having swept them up while Mads was trying to remind herself it was just a little blood. Georgia working while Mads fucked shit up.

Like usual.

And so not why she was here.

She needed to make this right, make it better.

"Let me grab that dust—"

Georgia wrapped her fingers around Mads's arm. From behind. Sending an immediate surge of panic through her. But instead of jerking away and shoving her off, instead of freaking out and injuring herself again, she froze, focused, *thought*.

Through the panic.

Progress.

"Here, honey," Georgia said, tearing open a bandage and smoothing it over her skin.

See? Georgia was being nice, and if Mads had freaked the fuck out, that would have been a whole other thing to make amends for and—

Her throat tightened as her pulse steadied and she processed what was happening.

What Georgia had done—*was* doing.

Only Ben had ever smoothed a Band-Aid on her skin. With gentle fingers.

Only Ben had bent over her skin and lightly brushed his lips over her hurts.

But Georgia did it then—

And froze, cheeks reddening. "I'm sorry," she said, pushing back her long, gray hair. "It's a force of habit."

"Don't—"

Mads's voice was a rasp that had Georgia freezing.

"Don't," she said again, pushing through the tightness in her throat. "Don't apologize. I just..." Mads exhaled. "I was just surprised is all."

Georgia slowly extended her hand again, wrapping it around Mads's and squeezing. "I'm sorry for the surprise all the same." Then she released Mads's hand and shuffled to the dustpan, bones practically creaking as she bent and picked up the scoop that was loaded with the broken pieces she'd already swept up.

Too much.

"Georgia—"

A look over her shoulder. "It's late, sweetie. You need to go home and rest. You work too hard."

A lie.

But the set of her frame told Mads there was no point in saying anything further.

"I'll get my jacket," she said softly as Georgia shuffled to the kitchen.

The pieces *clunked* into the trash as Mads snagged Ben's fleece and tugged it over her head. She grabbed her purse from the set of hooks in the front hall and hung it across her chest.

"I'm out of here—" she began, but Georgia's voice cut her off before she could finish her goodbye.

"I made you these." A paper bag was thrust in her direction.

Probably because Georgia was a lovely person, a sweet old lady that Mads cherished spending time with.

But she was an awful cook.

Mads took the bag—because she had no choice—and peeked inside. Oh, God.

There were cookies inside.

Cookies that should be delicious, should be something that couldn't possibly be ruined. Not in Georgia's world, though. Fluffy, gooey, chocolatey goodness was reduced to...

"Try one," Georgia encouraged. "I used a new recipe."

Shit.

She exhaled. "I'm actually—"

Georgia reached into the bag and the cookies bumping into each other sounded like...well, like hockey pucks *thunking* together in a bucket.

Her teeth hurt already. "I—"

"Try it," Georgia said, her sweet old lady smile so earnest that Mads found herself taking the cookie from her hand.

Lifting it to her mouth.

Already saliva pooled beneath her tongue, her taste buds objecting in preparation.

Why are you doing this to us? they protested.

But Georgia's puppy dog eyes were watching.

She opened her mouth, took a bite, and—

Sweet baby Jesus, that was as awful as anticipated. Somehow it was salty, but not in a sea salt caramel way. It was salty like a rogue wave had snuck up the beach and knocked her off her feet and another was right on its heels, breaking over her head, filling her mouth with briny water. Instantly, all moisture on her tongue dried up and her taste buds keened out a death cry and—

"What do you think?" Georgia asked with that damn earnest smile.

What did she think?

Death by cookie was a shitty ass way to go.

Worse, a gag was working its way up her throat—a gag she couldn't release. Not without hurting Georgia, and she'd done far too much of that already. She chewed the bite she'd taken (for approximately the hundredth time) and then swallowed painfully, the mixture sliding like already hardening concrete down her throat. "It's yummy," she rasped when she managed to get it down.

"Yay!" Georgia clapped her hands together, bouncing a little on her feet, looking more spry than Mads had ever seen her. "That's excellent news!"

She took the bag back and Mads released a silent sigh of relief.

Until Georgia kept talking. "I've got a whole other cookie sheet of them! Let me just top off your bag."

"Oh no," Mads began. "I—"

But Georgia was already gone, disappearing into the kitchen with the bag of cookies.

And reappearing only a couple of seconds later, the bag in her hand fuller. *Significantly* fuller. Something Mads felt intimately when Georgia passed the wrinkled brown paper sack back. Like bricks. Or that bucket of hockey pucks.

"Thanks," she said softly, folding down the top and holding it close.

They may be destined for her trash can when she got home, but she would never let Georgia see that, know that her efforts weren't appreciated so, *so* much.

After everything Mads had done...

Georgia was making her cookies.

The world was a strange, strange place.

"Get some sleep, sweetie," Georgia said, reaching past her and opening the door, pulling it open just enough for Mads to slip out.

They could never be too careful in this neighborhood.

"You too," she replied, pausing on the stoop to order. "Lock up."

The *click* hit her ears a moment later, and then she was walking down the cracked concrete path to her car, crammed into a tight street parking spot, always keeping her gaze moving, searching, making absolutely certain she was aware of her surroundings at all times.

She'd been in some tight and sketchy situations, but this neighborhood, especially after dark...well, she didn't want to be caught unaware—

One second she'd taken her gaze off the shadows and sidewalks and older, rundown houses to search her purse for her keys —a stupid mistake because she should have just gotten them out inside Georgia's house. But the damn cookies. She'd been thinking about them and not her keys.

Which she didn't find.

Because the next moment she was shoved back against her car door, a big, strong body pinning her in place.

Furious energy in the air.
Fear wracking her insides.
Panic freezing her in place.
Again.

EIGHT

LUCAS

She stilled so completely that he immediately froze, realized what he was doing.

The last time he'd grabbed her she'd panicked so intensely that she made herself *bleed*.

"Fuck," he hissed, and that seemed to snap her out of her stillness. She started fighting him and doing it *hard*.

"Let me go!" she yelled. "Let me *go!*"

"Shut up," he snapped, feeling like even more of an asshole than normal. But she was struggling and her eyes were panicked and he didn't want to hurt her—or draw any extra attention to them in this shitty ass neighborhood. "It's me," he said, gentling his tone slightly. But not completely because while he felt bad for scaring her, she was obviously up to no good and—

She blinked. "Lucas?"

"No shit."

Still dialed into asshole. Still unable to stop.

Because he'd cottoned on to what she was carrying—a crumpled brown bag.

Drugs.

She was here, shooting up or taking pills or however the fuck she liked to get high, and she was doing it knowing it would absolutely destroy her brother. Because that was what addicts did and that was what *users* did—hurt the people who loved them without giving one fuck who they mowed over in the process of seeking their own escape.

She blinked again. "*Lucifer?*" she snapped back. "What the fuck are you doing here?"

Stupid fucking nickname.

He ignored it, though, just lifting a brow. "What the fuck are *you* doing here?"

The anger in her eyes banked, shame crossing the deep brown.

Knew it. Fucking *knew* it.

And...he lost it. "You're pathetic, you know that, right? Doing this—being here when you know it's going to *kill* Ben to find out. Not to mention Jordyn and the boys. They love you for some fucking reason"—she flinched, but he was too far gone to really register the pain slicing across her face—"and you're here getting high. Fuck the kids you're supposedly helping"—he released his hold on her, mostly because he was ready to start shaking some sense into her and even though he may be an asshole, he drew the line at hurting women...physically anyway—"fuck the people who are relying on you and maybe looking to you for guidance. You just have to get hi—"

"Fuck you," she hissed, shoving him back with surprising strength.

He stumbled, righted himself.

But she was in his face again, lifting on tiptoe, jabbing a finger in his chest. "You know why I'm here?" Another jab. "You *know* why *I'm* here?"

"Yeah." He narrowed his eyes on the brown bag again. "I do."

She caught on this time, caught on that he knew what she was holding, her body going stiff.

But then she shocked the shit out of him because her mouth

curved up into a smirk. "Yeah, Lucifer"—she shoved the bag against his chest—"you know *exactly* why I'm here."

He'd caught the bag reflexively and it was heavier than he expected.

Must be a shit-ton of drugs in here.

Something he probably shouldn't be holding on the street, especially in this neighborhood. Something that—

"Aren't you going to open it?" she sneered. "To catch me in my lies and bad behavior?"

A thread of discomfort began to work itself through his stomach, but he ignored it as he peeled open the bag and began to rifle through the contents...

Then stared in disbelief at what he found.

"Yeah, asshole," she said, causing his head to jerk up. "They're cookies. *Only* cookies. Terrible tasting cookies that I accept from Georgia because I hurt her in the past and I will never do it again. I'll eat whatever awful recipe she cooks up because it's the l-least I can do."

Her eyes glimmered, evident with the faint glow of the moon, the stars overhead.

Her chest was rising and falling, her breaths in rapid gusts.

And he found he couldn't stand the silence.

"They can't be that bad," he said, reaching into the bag and pulling one out.

That had her eyes drying, her mouth curving up into that smirk he wanted to kiss off her lips again. "It's your funeral."

He lifted it to his nose, sniffed.

It smelled *mostly* like a normal cookie.

He took a bite—because of that smirk and those damp eyes and the tendrils—yup, they'd now become multiple—of guilt weaving their ways through his insides.

Not drugs. Cookies.

He was an ass—

"Fuck!" He just barely managed to avoid spitting out the bite he'd taken, a big one because he was an asshole with an ego who just *had* to prove to her they couldn't possibly be as bad as she made them seem.

In reality, it was worse.

Salt exploded on his tongue. Then just as his taste buds began to recover, something almost medicinal dominated his senses. It burned his tongue and filled his nose with...almonds? But maybe only in the barest sense of the word. Like something that had once been something that *resembled* almonds and the texture...

How did it somehow take a dozen chews to get through a single bite of cookie?

Her giggle snapped him out of the assault on his senses.

He'd never heard that up close before.

Across a room or yard while she was playing with Marcus, Sammy, and the other Gold kids, yeah. With Ben, when he murmured something in her ear while they sat side by side (and usually at the opposite end from him) in the booth at Mafia's, definitely. But a foot away, the soft puff of sound coating his skin? No. He'd never experienced that...

Pleasure?

No, that was fucking stupid, even allowing that thought to cross his mind.

She was Ben's sister, for one. For another, he'd been a complete and total asshole to her. Last, she was an addict and he wasn't going to touch that with a ten-foot pole. Too much of that in his past, his life, his—

"Can't be that bad, huh?" she asked, taking the bag back. "How's your tongue feeling?"

Terrible.

It felt fucking terrible.

But he wasn't going to admit that. "Fine," he muttered.

"And your conscience?" An arch question.

He froze.

"Exactly." She huffed and jammed the key into her car door, wrestling with the lock then struggling to tug the rusty, screeching metal panel wide. "That's what I thought," she muttered, tossing the bag onto the passenger's seat. "You don't have one, do you, Lucifer?"

He deserved that.

God knew he deserved far more fire than that.

And yet, he couldn't bring himself to apologize.

Because she could still turn out like...

Mentally shaking himself, he shrugged, lifting one shoulder and dropping it while saying disdainfully, "I'm not the one without a conscience."

That had her expression turning stricken.

And him feeling like a dick—rightfully—all over again. He sucked in a breath, knew he needed to stop with this shit, knew it wasn't fair, especially when it was *his* baggage that was continually coloring the way he interacted with her.

He needed to apologize.

But somehow, he couldn't go quite that far. "How did you hurt her?" he asked quietly.

Another flash of pain, more regret and worry and *asshole.* But she answered him. "I stole from Georgia's house," Mads said softly. "My dealer was in the neighborhood, and when I didn't have enough money to buy a hit, I'd..." An exhale. "I'd steal and sell it or trade it and"—her throat worked and she looked up at him with damp but steady eyes—"she caught me once. She could have called the cops. Instead, she told me to go and come back if I needed a safe place to stay."

Her lungs were sawing again.

"And before you ask," she murmured. "I stole from her over and over again. And she never called the police and she let me stay when I was too fucked up to leave and—" Her exhale was shuddering. "I hurt her. And she won't let me pay her back in actual money, so I bring her dinner once in a while and when I'm here, I clean and fix things and do my best to make it up to her. Because I was a fucking mess and a real bitch, and I spent far too long without a conscience...and this is the one small thing she'll allow me." Her throat worked, eyes hitting his. "And even still, sometimes I'll see her looking at the spot on her mantle that once held the antique clock that had belonged to her grandmother—the clock I pawned so I'd feel good for a couple of hours, so that I'd *forget* for a few hours—and I know I can never make it up to her." A beat of quiet.

"Because my conscience is heavy," Mads whispered. "So heavy that I'll never *ever* shed the guilt of the person I was."

Then she got in her car, slammed that screeching door, and drove away from him.

Again.

NINE

MADS

"Are you sure you're good?" Lily asked, having turned her fork sideways so she could use the tines to scrape up the minuscule amount of chocolate syrup remainingon her plate.

They were eating fluffy pancakes.

Or *had* eaten them anyway.

Fluffy pancakes simply being her and Lily's name for the soufflé goodness that came in pancake form and was topped with all manner of deliciousness.

More often than not, Mads went for the Peach Persuasion variety—fresh peaches and homemade whipped cream topped with a freeze-dried peachy crumble—while Lily skipped around the menu like the flittering beautiful jumping bean she was, trying new combinations on the fly.

Bright and sweet and flitting around.

Taking on projects. Fixing people.

Including Mads.

Befriending her when she'd wanted to be left alone, pulling her out of the guilt that regularly ate her alive.

"I'm good," Mads said, forcing her tone to remain light. "I'm mostly just in awe of your ability to devour each and every molecule of fluffy pancakes."

Lily narrowed her eyes. "I'm just making sure I'm not being wasteful."

"Is that what they call licking your plate nowadays?"

Now Lily's mouth was curving. "And if I say yes?"

"Then I say more power to you."

Lily giggled, took one more scrape of her fork and lifted it to her mouth, licking off what had to amount to a minuscule amount of chocolate mousse.

Mads loved a fluffy pancake, but she wasn't a chocolate girl, wasn't really a dessert girl at all—with the fluffy pancakes being one of the few exceptions. And that was mostly because she got to do it sitting across from the person who knew her, warts and all, and didn't look at her like she was a broken person who hurt everyone around her.

Unlike...Luc—

"Mads."

She mentally shook herself and forced a smile, and even though she was barely half finished with her stack of pancakes, her appetite had disappeared, the portion she'd eaten so far sitting heavy on her stomach, the sweet residue on her tongue cloying and overpowering.

She set her fork on her plate, sat back.

"*Mads.*"

"I'm fine," she said softly. Finally able to force her eyes to Lily's, she kept her forced smile in place by pure dint.

Waste of an effort.

Because Lily saw right through her anyway.

"You're a good person."

That sliced, deep and hard, and not even because of the fierce way that Lily said it, but because it *shouldn't* have sliced. It was a nice thing to say...

And it made her feel like shit.

Because she might be a nice person right now, but for too long she hadn't—

"Stop it."

The hissed-out order had her jumping, and then Lily took Mads's hand, squeezing hard enough that her knuckles protested and she winced, but the slight vein of pain cleared some of the haze from her brain, the same cloud that had sat heavy on her shoulders, weighing her down ever since...

She'd gotten sober.

Maybe longer.

"Feelings aren't facts," Lily said, still fiercer and more intense than Mads had ever heard, even when Lily was kicking her now-fiancé's ass for being...well, an *ass*.

"I know that," she said, keeping her voice soft.

A lie.

Which Lily called her on. "Bullshit!" She squeezed again, though not as hard this time. Because Lily didn't knowingly hurt someone, and of course she'd tracked the fact that Mads had winced the first go around. "You had a heap full of shit tossed on your plate for years and years and *years*. You have trauma and lost a lot and you've been hurt *too* much."

"I—"

"You tried to numb your pain in the wrong way and yes, you hurt your brother, but the thing is, Mads, we all fuck up, we all make mistakes. The important thing is how we try to right our wrongs."

She inhaled.

"Sometimes we stumble while trying to fix our fuckups." Lily squeezed again. "But the most important thing is *how* we move forward."

Mads's lips parted, her breath sliding out in a quiet hiss.

"And to *keep* moving forward," Lily said, gentle now. "To keep putting one foot in front of the other."

Mads was trying to do that, trying to make up for all she'd

done, trying to rebuild some of the bridges she'd so dramatically burned—

"But that doesn't mean sacrificing yourself in the process." Another squeeze. "Or to continue beating yourself up," Lily added softly. "Since you're really good at that too."

"I have a lot to make up for," she murmured.

"And what?" Lily pulled back her hand, and Mads hated the sense of loss, of aloneness, like she'd pushed her friend too far and now was going to lose her.

But she *didn't* lose her.

Lily stood—making her heart thump hard, but only for a second. Because then her friend was rounding the table and squeezing onto the bench next to Mads, wrapping an arm around her shoulders.

"Let me ask you this," Lil said softly. "If you saw one of your kids treating herself like this, would you let it slide?"

"That's not the same."

Lily touched her cheek. "Isn't it?"

Mads inhaled, ready to protest, but stopped because...

She *wouldn't* let one of her kids continue to beat themselves up. "But..."

"Stop right there, honey," Lily said gently. "Just sit in the moment before you start working up a protest because you feel like you *have* to protest."

Mads closed her mouth.

"That's it," Lily encouraged. "Sit in that feeling and take that little bit of progress."

Sighing, Mads shook her head. "You make it sound so easy."

"It's not."

Said so baldly that Mads blinked at Lily's tone.

Then chuckled.

Because...that was Lily. Her friend. Her friend who didn't pull any punches.

"So, just sit in the little bits of growth," Lily went on. "Accept them and keep moving forward. And accept my ass-kickings when you fuck up."

"It's that simple?"

Lily grinned then dropped her head onto Mads's shoulder, tone sobering. "I wish I could make this easier for you."

Mads settled the side of her head on top of Lily's, sighing. "Is this where you say I have to be patient because I'm undoing a lot of years of bullshit?"

"I couldn't say it better myself."

Mads highly doubted that.

But she accepted the compliment anyway.

Look at her go.

Progress.

She hadn't managed to finish her pancakes, but because Lily had declared that the crime of the century, her friend had taken one for the team and ate the rest of her Peach Persuasion.

Now she was driving back to her apartment, ready for her bath and book time.

Ready to sit in that feeling of progress.

Only when she turned the corner, happening to pass by the youth center on her way home, gaze searching the shadows like always, did that progress turn to panic.

Because of the lone figure walking, head and shoulders bowed, hoodie engulfing her slender body, stride quick.

Like she wanted to go unnoticed.

But Mads recognized her immediately.

She pulled over to the side of the road, rolling down her window. "Olivia!"

The girl froze, but just for a second before starting to walk faster.

"Shit," Mads muttered, shutting off the engine, opening the door, and running after Olivia. "Vivi, wait!"

That slowed her kiddo down enough that Mads was able to

catch up to her, to get in front of her. "Hey, hey," she said, careful not to touch her. "What's going on?"

Olivia's makeup was in streaks down her cheeks, black mascara in half-moons beneath her eyes. "Nothing," she said sullenly.

Man, the kid wasn't even making a good effort.

"Vivi, come on," Mads said. "Don't try that shit with me."

"I—"

For a moment Mads thought that Olivia would continue with the lie, and a bolt of hurt shot through her middle at the idea. They'd been building a friendship for a long time, and if Vivi didn't trust her—

"I had a fight with my mom."

Mads's pulse sped up. "Yeah?"

"She's got a new boyfriend, and he's a total dick!" she burst out. "He, like, makes her cook and clean all the time, and he threw a bottle at her the other day. She had to get stitches."

Fuck.

"Is he hurting you?"

Olivia froze, probably because Mads's tone was deadly. "No," she whispered.

"Is he there now?"

A nod. "I'm going to my dad's."

Mads glanced around the darkened street. "*Now?*"

Vivi shrugged. "My mom wouldn't drive me."

"Wouldn't or couldn't?"

A flash of emotion across Vivi's face and Mads knew that it was both. She wanted to press, wanted to go to Olivia's mom's house and rain down hellfire. But it was late and Vivi was clearly upset and...her kiddo had a safe space to go.

"Come on," Mads said instead of pressing.

"What?" Vivi asked.

"I'll drive you to your dad's."

TEN

LUCAS

Rome sat down next to him with a sigh. "You ready for the grind?"

Considering Lucas had done nothing but work out, eat right, and think about hockey for the majority of this off-season, he felt more than ready.

Maybe more ready than he'd ever been.

But being ready didn't fill in the giant hole inside him.

Maybe less hole than a huge writhing mass of guilt.

He owed a certain woman an apology—and he knew that no matter how grand that apology was it wouldn't be enough.

Because part of him was still waiting.

For her to fuck up.

And that made him even more of an asshole than he'd previously thought.

His baggage was clouding hers, and he didn't know which way was up, which thoughts were his own and which were because of his past. He didn't even know how to start thinking about that, didn't know if he *could* think about it.

Fucking shit all twisted up.

So maybe he was physically ready for the season, but his mind was a goddamned mess.

And this wasn't the time to think about it.

He had to get his focus on the sport, on his team, and off the woman who'd looked at him with such hurt in her eyes over a bag of cookies.

Cleaning for a woman named Georgia, not wanting to hurt her feelings over shitty cooking.

Legos and books.

Running with the kids on the grass, hugging her brother tight, watching out for Lily.

The way the kids at the youth center looked at her, followed her around.

So maybe it was less twisted mess of remorse and more...he needed to get the fuck out of his own head and see the truth in front of him.

"Dude."

Lucas blinked at the hard nudge that accompanied the word, saw that he'd wrapped his shin guard and sock with about an entire roll of clear tape.

Jesus Christ.

He tore the roll, moved to his other leg, using an appropriate amount of tape this time.

"I'm guessing you're less ready for hockey than I thought."

Despite being in the best shape of his life, Lucas couldn't disagree with him. "I'm fine," he lied. "And I'm ready for the grind—or as ready as we always are."

"I hear that." Rome bent to tighten his skate. "But we'll get through and kick ass in the process—"

The locker room door flew open.

"I'm back, bitches!"

Lucas's head jerked up and his brows dragged together when he put the voice to the figure walking through the opening.

The *retired* player.

Who was carrying her leg pads slung over one shoulder and her helmet tucked under one arm.

"Umm," Rome said softly.

Josh jumped up, huge smile on his face. "Brit! You filling in for Koslov today?" Their former backup goalie had been delayed by some overseas travel complications.

Brit's mouth curved up, and her blond ponytail flew as she shook her head. "Funny story, but Koslov decided he wasn't coming back."

That had the locker room falling quiet.

"Umm," Rome said again, still soft.

"So that means you're stuck with me for one more season, bitches!" She plunked her helmet onto the bench, did a little dance—her characteristic Brit happy dance, really. "I signed the contract about five minutes ago."

The room was silent.

For Lucas's part, it came from shock. He'd already come to terms with the fact that they would be losing one of the strongest personalities on the roster, the woman who had become the backbone of the team. There would be a hole, and it was their responsibility to figure out how to fill it.

That was their job.

But now it seemed like they didn't have to do that?

Because Brit was here for the season?

What about Roxie and Stefan and the plans she'd been talking about? Was this why her retirement party had been canceled, the date it was supposed to be rescheduled as yet to be determined?

And why did she seem happy...but not?

He glanced at Rome, wondered if his friend and teammate saw what he was seeing.

That Brit might be smiling and doing a little dance.

But she didn't seem truly, bone-deep happy.

Rome shook his head, telling Lucas he didn't get it either, but by then, the rest of the locker room had unstuck and the guys had gathered around Brit, some were hugging her, others punching her arms and giving her shit about holding out on them. Coop ruffled her hair and shook his head, grin wide as he muttered something that Lucas couldn't hear from where he was, but it made Brit laugh loud and long and *that* sounded happy.

That was the Brit he knew.

He waded through the guys, tugged on the end of her ponytail, then took his turn to hug her when she glanced up at him, wrapping his arms around her and whispering in her ear, "Is this what you meant about being confused?"

She stilled.

Then drew back, something in her chocolate eyes he didn't like.

But it was gone in an instant, her trademark grin in place. "Let's just say I'm not confused any longer."

He narrowed his eyes, opened his mouth—

Just as Coach strode into the room. "All right, boys and Brit" —a sentiment that never failed to make Lucas's lips twitch because Brit felt like one of the boys and to bother making the distinction was ridiculous, but he wasn't Coach and he wasn't Brit, so he just let it amuse him and moved on—"Enough chattering. Get dressed and get focused and get your asses on the ice."

That broke apart the rest of the huddles, everyone going to their respective stalls to finish gearing up.

Then they got on the ice.

But even though Brit said all the right things and looked like she'd never missed a day on the ice, Lucas couldn't forget her smile.

Because it was wrong.

———

He was an idiot.

A total fucking idiot.

He'd heard Ben and Josh talking about going to the youth

center to help with a paint program Mads was doing with the kids that night.

Now he was there.

Or rather, he'd helped out during the paint party—and now had the gold glitter-covered sneakers to prove it—and he'd done it avoiding the glare of Mads, avoiding *Lucifer*.

Probably because he'd avoided being a dick.

Go him.

But, now instead of going home, instead of allowing the tough practice and exhaustion that was pulling at his mind and body to take him home, to take him to bed, he was sitting in his car. In the dark.

In the parking lot of the youth center.

Waiting for Mads.

Only for once, it wasn't waiting for her to fuck up.

It was to...

Watch her.

Which, right, didn't sound much better—it had significantly less asshole, but was a lot more creepy.

"You're a fucking idiot," he muttered, tearing his gaze from the front doors of the youth center, from where he'd hoped to get a glimpse of Mads—because he was said idiot—and leaned forward to jab at the button to start up his car.

But just as his finger grazed the button, Mads came out.

And she wasn't alone.

A girl was at her side, fragile and frail and looking like one stiff breeze would push her over. She hung near Mads as she locked up, seeming to not want to leave. Mads didn't appear bothered, chatting with the girl in a way that told him they'd had many conversations, many interactions just like this.

Then the doors were locked and they were headed toward Mads's car. The girl started to round the hood to get into the passenger's seat—

And froze, hand on the handle, mouth open, head whipping around.

A second later, she was running, disappearing into the shadows, out of sight faster than Lucas would have thought possible.

Mads's voice echoed through the windows, a shout that reached his ears even as the actually words she'd called were indiscernible.

He reached for the door handle and was stepping out of his car before he processed moving.

ELEVEN

MADS

One second, she and Vivi were discussing the painting class she wanted to enroll Vivi in and the next, the girl was sprinting away, disappearing into the darkness of the night, the passenger side car door swinging noisily.

She straightened from where she'd bent to lean across the console and manually disengage the lock on the passenger's door.

Because her car was that old.

Vivi!" she shouted, watching the girl take off.

But it was too late.

The girl was gone and Mads was left with a pounding heart and a loudly screeching door and—

She gasped—a man strolling across the parking lot.

The memories flooded through her in a rush, smacking so hard that she found herself skittering back a step, her insides knotting tightly. Bile burned the back of her throat and for a second, she seriously thought she was going to throw up.

But then she got angry.

Really fucking *angry*.

He was *here*, at the youth center, striding casually up to her with that fucking smirk on his face. A smirk that had been pointed toward the shadows, the darkness in which Vivi had disappeared...and was now directed at Mads.

A face that had once brought her bliss and oblivion.

Drugs and sex.

Sex *for* drugs. Sex because she wanted to feel accepted.

Sex because she wanted to feel nothing when the drugs and booze weren't enough.

And now he was strolling across the parking lot.

Her temple throbbed, and she lifted her hand, touching the small spot at her hairline, the slender raised line that came from a bottle being thrown...by the very man who was now only a few feet away.

She should have known when Vivi said her mom got stitches from a bottle. Should have put the pieces together. It was just too much of a coincidence.

Except—

How *could* she have known?

It wasn't like Nick held the monopoly on bottle launching. Men hurt women all the time—as she'd experienced over and over and *over* again. It was just that Nick was an extra special brand of asshole. He made Lucas and his slicing barbs, his quiet confrontations behind her brother's back, seem like support of the greatest magnitude.

"Madeline."

She shuddered and hated that he saw it.

But *God*, she fucking despised that name.

And that had her anger growing, far eclipsing the fear, the guilt for not making the connection between the bottle and Vivi's shitty living situation—her mom and a man who could be none other than Nick, if just for where Vivi's mom's lived and the dark shit she was into and what had brought Vivi to the fucking youth center in the first place. It wasn't for the fucking art classes and hockey players. It was because it was a safe space for her and that Mads hadn't recognized exactly the kind of danger Vivi was in...

Killed.

Thankfully, Mads's rage was blooming and it swallowed all of that—though she knew it would emerge to sink its claws into her mind at some point in the future, probably late at night when she was trying to sleep and the urge to numb ate at her.

Right now, it was tucked away.

And she was *fucking pissed.*

"What are you doing here?" she snapped.

His mouth curved up, and there was no way that a man so beautiful should be so fucking evil. But this was reality and life wasn't fair. *That* was why he was there. "My dear, dear Madeline," he began, reaching out to touch her.

"No," she snapped, smacking at his hand and lurching back.

But her car was right there.

And in an instant, she was pinned between a hard male body and the cool metal of her car.

Inanely, some part of her recognized that this wasn't like being pinned by Lucas that night last week. He'd come close. He'd startled her. But his hands had also protected her from colliding hard with the steel, from being hurt.

Clearly, Nick had no such desire.

He moved fast and abruptly, ramming her back against her car, sending pain up and down her spine. A heartbeat later his hand was in her hair, clenching at the strands on her nape. Fire on her scalp, shooting down through her neck. Then he gripped her jaw with his other hand, digging in hard enough that all the other hurts caught up with her and her eyes began to water.

"You little bitch," he snapped. "You don't tell me *no.*"

It would be easy to wilt, to become the woman she'd been less than two years before.

But...she wasn't.

And that was why she jerked her head, dislodging his palm

from her jaw. She shoved against his chest and kicked out at him and managed...

To gain a few inches.

For a few seconds.

Because then his hand in her hair tightened, yanking her head back, and if she'd thought she had fire in her scalp before, that had just been the slightest of sparks. Now it was a fucking inferno blasting through her nerve endings, sending her watering eyes straight to gushing, hot tears pouring down her cheeks, dripping off her jaw and soaking into her shirt.

And then his fist was descending, almost in slow motion.

She saw it getting closer, closer, *close*—

An explosion of pain, her vision going hazy, pain upon pain upon *pain*.

There was a noise—a scuffle and then the cold hit her, Nick's weight, Nick's brutal hands leaving her in an instant.

She collapsed to the ground, the pavement biting into her palms, her forearms, just breathing through the hurts, waiting for them to recede. And when they finally did, when she could see clearly, it was to find Lucas standing over Nick, shaking out his fist while Nick scooted away, feet scrabbling for purchase on the ground.

Oh, shit.

Lucas was going to kill him.

She must have made some sort of noise—perhaps fueled by the fact that she was about to have a hockey player's career-ending actions (assault and battery didn't exactly mesh with an NHLer's honor clause in their contract)—because Lucas froze, his head whipping around, his eyes fixing on hers.

It was dark.

But she still saw into his very soul.

The rage. The guilt. The fear. The—

Nick finally managed to get his feet beneath him, boots scuffing against the pavement.

Lucas clenched the hand he'd been shaking back into a fist, took a step toward Nick—

"No," she whispered.

But he heard her, stopping, turning back, eyes coming to hers again. This time they were shuttered though, that glimpse into his soul gone.

Nick skittered back another step, and her gaze went there. She took in his face, knew that she hadn't seen the last of him, that he really wouldn't take well to Lucas having gotten the better of him. But he was also a coward.

He wouldn't make that move now.

He'd wait until she was alone and vulnerable and—

Lucas started walking toward her.

She *wasn't* alone.

And she was going to make it so she wasn't vulnerable. Not ever again.

Lucas crouched in front of her, finger coming to her chin, gently—oh so gently—coaxing it up. "Mads," he murmured.

That unlocked something in her and she scrambled up to her feet. "I'm fine. I—"

She wavered, nearly fell to the pavement a second time, her head spinning, vision blurring.

"Easy, Peaches," came Lucas's gentle voice. "You're okay now."

"I—"

Thirty seconds ago, she'd promised herself that she wasn't going to be vulnerable, and now she didn't know if she was going to pass out or throw up.

And *Lucas* was holding her steady, keeping her upright with an arm around her shoulders, slowly drawing her closer to his chest, keeping her near enough that she could scent him, could feel the heat of him, could hear the rapid *thrum-thrum, thrum-thrum* of his heart pounding against his rib cage.

Maybe she should have pushed away, shouldn't have allowed

herself that moment of comfort—of *vulnerability*—given by the man who despised her.

But also thirty seconds before, she'd promised herself she wasn't alone.

And Lucas, with his arms around her, with the steady beat of his pulse in her ears, made her think...

She wasn't.

At least for a few minutes.

TWELVE

Lucas

She was trembling.

And had tried to push away from him a half-dozen times in the last five minutes, saying, "I'm fine."

But she was *trembling*.

He had no right to be holding her, no right to feel like some of the jagged edges of his soul were buffed out, smoothed over.

But...she was trembling.

Under the stars and nearly full moon with the cool crisp air of fall clinging to his skin, and doing it in his arms—

"I'm fine," she whispered again, and since she pushed a little harder, didn't waver on her feet when he loosened his hold, he had no reason to continue keeping her against him. No reason except for the embers blossoming in his stomach.

The clarity that had slowly been growing over the last couple of days.

Him—asshole.

Her—not what he'd thought.

Him—big, giant asshole (mentioned twice, just for good measure).

"I'm—"

She wavered again, nearly went down, and he caught her against him again. "All right," he said softly. "I think you need to go to the hospital."

The fucker had punched her—the bruise was already blooming on her face—and head injuries were no joke. He knew guys whose careers had ended because of an odd-timed hit, a crash into the boards, a fight gone wrong.

"I'm fine," she said again. "Really, I'm—" She broke off, hand lifting to the unbruised side of her head.

Not fine. She wasn't fine at all—

She heaved.

Vomit splattered on his shirt, his pants, his shoes, and her face, if he wasn't so fucking worried about her, her expression was almost fucking comical.

"Oh, my God," she said, clamping a hand over her mouth. "I'm so sorry—"

"Right, then." He bent, snagged her purse, tucking it beneath his arm on the unsoiled side of his body. He wrapped his other arm around her when she wavered again, started to lead her back to his SUV.

"My car," she said halfway there.

He glanced up, registered the passenger side door sitting halfway open. "If anyone steals that rust bucket POS that's your car, they're an idiot."

Mads tried to turn back, fighting his hold. "It's *my* car."

Christ.

"I'll go lock it up, okay? Let's get you settled in my car first, yeah?"

Worry on her face, her brows drawn tight and her lips pressing flat.

"I'll go back," he told her. "I promise."

Protest in her eyes, but then her lids slid closed, her weight coming against him more heavily. "Fine," she eventually muttered. "But if it gets stolen because you don't, I'll never forgive you."

"Add it to my tab." He tugged at the handle, opened the door for her. "God knows that I've given you a long ass list already."

He'd been helping her down onto the seat, but that had her freezing, gaze coming back to his.

Pretty brown eyes.

Russet brows drawn together.

Pink lips parting.

His cock twitched—and seriously, how fucked up was he that his dick had finally decided to work now? Going chub while he was covered in vomit and about to escort a probably concussed woman to the hospital.

"I don't blame you," she whispered.

His mouth curved. "Is that why you call me Lucifer?" A blip of regret across her face, so he hurried to add, "I earned that, Peaches. All on my own." He nudged her into motion again. "Now let me buckle you in—"

Her fingers wrapped around his wrist. "I don't blame you." Another whisper.

He touched her cheek. Lightly. Barely allowing his skin to come in contact with the silken softness of hers. "I do. I'm an asshole and I let my past hurt you and I'm sorry."

Her mouth dropped open.

And his cock twitched again.

Seriously. Fucked. Up.

"Lucas—"

He buckled her belt, straightened up, and careful to not smack the back of his idiotic head as he maneuvered out of his car. "I'll be right back," he said, passing over her purse. Then he was closing her door, hustling back across the parking lot and locking up her car.

"Thank you," she whispered as he climbed into the driver's seat.

"I just hope you have your keys," he told her as he pulled out of the lot. "Because I locked up but didn't check to see if they were floating around your car before I closed the door."

"I have them," she whispered, holding up a hand, opening her fingers, and showing him a set of keys.

"Good."

Silence fell between them, only the quiet rumble of road noise reaching his ears.

He searched for something to say.

And failed.

So, he just kept his mouth shut and drove her to the hospital.

It was the first smart thing he did with this woman.

———

"I should call your brother," he said several hours later, after tests and ice packs, pain meds and an interview with a police officer, along with an argument about filing for a restraining order (she said that wouldn't make a difference, he and the officer said she needed to do it anyway—something she'd acquiesced to).

Now she was almost sitting in the passenger's seat of his SUV, her lush ass hovering a couple of inches from the leather. "Don't," she said.

"Mads," he warned.

"I'll tell him in the morning, I promise. I just..." Her throat worked. "Let him sleep tonight, yeah?"

If he had a sister who wasn't a total fucking train wreck bitch with an evil streak a mile wide (which *both* his sisters were—something he'd finally figured out like the dumbass he was, that Mads *wasn't*, not by a long shot), he'd want to know right now. Hell, he would have wanted to know hours before. Would have been pissed to not have received an immediate phone call.

Ben was going to beat his ass.

And Lucas would deserve it—for a multitude of reasons.

But looking at Mads's face right then, seeing the bleakness in her expression, as though she knew exactly what he'd say—and that it would be fuck no, he was calling Ben right that moment— had him unable to say the words.

"Okay, Peaches," he said instead.

Her face changed, eyes not exactly soft at the edges, but maybe not quite so forlorn. "Thanks," she whispered, the surprise in her tone a punch in the gut.

He'd earned that.

"Let's get you home."

Throat working, she nodded, whispered again, "Thanks."

He drew the belt across her, doing it slowly so as not to make her flinch, something easing inside him when she didn't. He didn't deserve that, deserved to have the fucking twisted, spiked mass of guilt that was eating away at his insides forever.

He'd made her flinch before. Made her face cloud with hurt.

Fuck, he was an *asshole*.

He bit back a sigh, eyes sliding closed.

But they flew open when fingers pressed lightly against his jaw.

"What's the matter?" Mads asked, those soft fingertips searing into his skin.

"I'm an asshole."

She blinked, mouth dropping open slightly, surprise sending her cheeks just the slightest bit pink.

"I'm an asshole and I misjudged you," he rasped. "And I'm so *so* sorry."

Then, slowly, so as to avoid that flinch, to avoid hurting her, to avoid scaring her, he covered her fingers with his own.

So slender and fragile.

Breakable.

But also, something that was able to be healed.

Case in point, her saying—not whispering, *saying*, "You were an asshole. A big one, Lucifer"—now it was *his* turn to flinch— "but if I've learned anything, it's that everyone deserves a second

—or third, or *fourth*"—her lips turned up, showing him the steel beneath the broken but glued back together pieces—"chance."

"Mads."

"It's what you do with those chances that really shows who you are inside."

Thirteen

Mads

I t had taken her a long time to fall asleep the previous night, and it wasn't worry about Vivi and Nick that had kept her up.

That *should* have made sleep an elusive creature, should have had her stomach churning and her mind spinning.

Instead, she'd struggled to keep her mind off deep blue eyes that had swirled with grief, a voice that was full a remorse. A scent that was pure man—spicy and dark with hints of citrus.

How the heat of his body had felt when he'd carried her from her car and into his, but also the pure warmth that radiated from his body anytime he was near.

But most of all...she struggled to keep her mind off The Apology.

The most sincere apology she'd ever been on the receiving end of, full of remorse and pain and sadness in those blue, *blue* eyes.

And...

He'd just given it.

Because he'd misjudged her and seen that she wasn't who he thought and...

That fact had settled deep in her belly.

In her heart.

"It was one apology, Mads," she said softly as she pushed out of bed, tired of thinking about The Apology and Lucas and all the mistakes she'd made. And since she didn't want to think about Nick and the restraining order she needed to go down to the police station to file or worry about Vivi, she knew she just needed to get her ass out from under the covers, shower, and get her butt in gear.

She'd deal with the hard stuff like she always did.

One step at a time.

Exhaling, she tossed the covers back, moved to the bathroom, shrugging into her cozy robe—it was made out of some fake polyester blend that was softer than sin and would probably go up in flames at the tiniest bit of contact with heat, but she loved it.

The way it felt on her skin.

The warmth it settled over her body.

She'd spent so many nights feeling cold, shivering under the night air, clothes damp and wet hair soaking into her shirt. To feel warm and secure and something soft on her skin was a luxury that she would never take for granted.

Not ever again.

Sighing, she picked up her toothbrush and got down to business with brushing her teeth and carefully washing her face. A spritz of dry shampoo because there was no fucking way she was going to bother with washing—and then *drying*—her hair. She ran her fingers through it, wrapped it up into a messy bun, and then put on some light makeup.

That became much less light when she tried to cover up the dark bruise on her cheek and temple.

"Jesus," she muttered, having just finished fighting with hiding the scrape and then the bright pink line from her run-in with the car door, and now she not only had a re-injured temple, but also a blooming bruise on her cheek and around her eye.

She could slather on concealer for the next century and she wouldn't be any closer to covering up the bruise.

Ben was going to freak.

Margie, the head of the youth center, was going to freak.

Lily was going to freak.

A whole bunch of hockey players who'd taken her under their wings for inexplicable reasons were going to freak.

And...well, it wasn't annoying.

She understood very well that she'd been a burden for too long, but she'd also been without care for a long time. A lot of it was her own doing...but a lot of it wasn't. So, to feel like she was part of something, part of a family—

Good.

Bottom line was, it made her feel good, whether or not she'd come to terms with deserving it.

She dabbed on another layer of concealer, sighed at the hopelessness of it, and was just turning for her dresser (swapping her cozy robe for adult clothes was always the last thing she did getting ready) when the doorbell rang.

She paused, gaze going to the clock then to the door, as though she had X-ray vision and could see through the wood to whoever was on the other side.

Nick?

The police?

Lucas?

Ben?

None of whom she was ready to deal with.

Two of whom were scary—Nick and the police. The first because duh. The second because she'd been seriously fucked up and had broken lots of laws and had lived with the police-equals-bad mentality branded into her mind for too long. She knew there were good ones, but she also knew there were bad ones—because she'd personally dealt with them and had the horror stories etched into her brain.

Exhaling, because that wasn't her life now, because she was

moving on and finding her worth and making her amends and coming to terms with the fact that she was an imperfect person who was doing her best to be a decent human being now, she turned for the door.

Peep through the peephole.

Then decide how she'd deal with them.

But her inner waffling meant that the person on the other side of the door got impatient.

Because the bell went again and this time it was accompanied by loud knocking on the door. Well, less knocking and more a pounding fist that threatened to break through the wood.

Or *maybe* her imagination was out of control.

Or *maybe* her trauma was speaking.

Because the pounding brought up...

A person she didn't want to think about.

"Enough, Mads," she whispered. "It's not him." It couldn't be him. He'd gone to jail and he hadn't come out, murdered in what officials had called an "unfortunate accident," but what she hoped was a form of jailhouse justice.

Either way, she was probably a bad person because she found more than a little peace in knowing he wouldn't get out, wouldn't come back and hurt her again.

The knocking cut off, reminding her that she needed to get her shit together and at least look through the peephole.

Tightening the tie on her robe, she moved quietly through the door while trying to calm her mind.

It couldn't be Nick.

For one, he didn't know where she lived.

For another, he was an opportunist. He didn't persist in anything that took longer than two minutes. Take advantage, milk a situation to its fullest potential, and then move on to suck the life out of someone else.

It could be the police or Ben or Lucas, she supposed. Though she figured Lucas was the least likely since he'd done his good dead of the century with his heroics last night.

If anything, he'd probably called Ben and now her brother was on the other side of the door and about to lose his shit on her because she hadn't immediately called—

Considering her apartment wasn't very large, she'd reached the door and was bending to glance through the peephole.

Which meant that she nearly jumped out of her skin when the knock came again.

"Fuck," she whispered, clamping a hand to her chest, heart racing. Only now a thread of annoyance had sewn itself through her insides, pulled itself tight.

It was the middle of the morning.

She wasn't expecting visitors.

The least they could do was give a woman a minute.

Sighing, she bent, completed her glancing through the peephole.

And that single thread of annoyance multiplied into a million.

FOURTEEN

LUCAS

He ran a hand through his still-damp hair and walked out into the lobby of the rink.

It was just after lunch hour on a weekday, so the space wasn't crowded. A few diehards playing pickup hockey and a couple of figure skating regulars were occupying the various sheets of ice. Of which there were five at the Gold's practice facility—four dedicated for the community, a fifth the Gold themselves got first dibs on. That didn't mean it was solely reserved for their use—it was on rotation for the rec leagues and tournaments and even visiting NHL teams.

The Gold and their players just got priority.

Case in point, he and Brit, Coop and Rome and Ben all getting in a little extra ice time.

Brit had arranged it, said she needed a tune-up with her retirement-now-back-to-playing-one-more-season shenanigans.

When in actuality, she looked like she'd never missed a day on the ice.

Somehow growing quicker as the years went by. Definitely more confident and relaxed in her position. And she'd won, what?

Three Cups? That was bound to make a person understand the value they brought to a team.

So, all that being said, he and Ben, Rome and Coop were mostly there just to fuck around and watch Brit put them all to shame.

Grinning, he inhaled the scent of the rink, that mix of hockey gear and concessions, of cold, crisp air and the slightly damp note of fog creeping in from outside. Showers and popcorn. Video games, cleaning products, propane from the ice resurfacers. It was part nostalgia, part too many kids with sticky fingers and who didn't like to shower and dudes who didn't wash their gear, like ever.

It wasn't like the Gold Mine, the carefully curated lights and odors and sounds. The fans in gold and black jerseys.

That was great.

Hell, that was fucking awesome.

It was his dream.

But...*this?* It was his past, his escape, his path to survival. It was his *life*, his *love*, his—

"Uh-*hum.*"

He blinked, realized he was standing in the middle of the lobby, eyes on the center rink, lost in his head.

"*Uh-hum.*"

The throat clearing was louder this time. And closer.

He spun, saw that Mads was standing there, looking pissed, complete with her arms crossed and her foot tapping on the ground.

"Mads?" he asked inanely, considering she was right there in front of him, doing all of that throat clearing and foot tapping and arm crossing.

She huffed out a breath, dropped her arms to her side.

Or one of them anyway.

Because the other lifted, hand fisting with the exception of her pointer finger, which jabbed him right in the chest. "What the fuck do you think you're doing?"

"Um…" His gaze flicked back to the center rink. He wasn't about to tell her he was standing there feeling nostalgic about playing in shitty rundown rinks growing up, practically living at his local one, using practice and games as an excuse to get away from home, taking advantage of any coaching, any free ice time, any chance to forget about his family and do something he liked for a change. Picking up odd jobs like putting new laces in the rental skates or eventually learning how to run the sharpening machine. Anything that would keep him at the rink longer.

Surviving on whatever food the snack bar guy would give him for a couple of bucks—or for free, more often than not.

God, if Lucas thought back with the knowledge of an adult, knowing what he knew now, he'd never really bought a meal, not even close with those couple of bucks that somehow always made their way back into his hockey bag or backpack.

But he couldn't share that shit with Mads.

She had enough to deal with.

Her brows flicked up sharply, and he blinked again, forced himself to focus. "What am I doing?"

For once, he wasn't being an asshole. He hadn't called Ben, had left that to Mads to do, and—

"You're really going to play dumb about the locksmith who showed up at my front door this morning?" It was a dangerous, arch question.

She had a shit lock.

He'd noticed that when he'd dropped her off the night before, wanting to stay longer and make sure she was okay, but not having any reason to.

So, he'd decided to do something about her shitty lock that wouldn't stop a fly. It wasn't a big thing, paying for a new dead bolt that would actually keep someone out— especially a *someone* she was going to file a restraining order against.

But she was standing there looking pissed.

And he was genuinely confused. Unless—

"Did they come too early?" he asked. "I told them that you

had a late night and to not come until after ten..." He trailed off when he caught sight of her expression. Which was swiveling between rage and confusion, and if he wasn't mistaken, more than a little bemusement. "What?" he asked after a moment.

"I come here pissed about a locksmith and you're assuming it's because *he came too early?*"

"Um..." Well, now he knew that was the wrong answer. "No?"

She dropped back onto her heels, and he immediately hated the distance. "No," she said, her annoyance seeming to freeze in place, to maybe recede a little as her head cocked to the side and she studied him for one long moment. "Why'd you send the locksmith, Lucas?"

His heart thudded hard just once, his throat grew thick. Then he managed to speak. "Your lock was shit." A shrug. "You need to be safe." Especially with fuckers on the loose who might find out where she lived and come after her.

Her nostrils flared on an inhale, the sharp puff of air loud in the quiet between them. "I—"

She shook her head, lips clamping together.

"What?" he asked.

"It doesn't matter." She turned like she was going to go and he'd moved before he processed taking that first step, moving around her, standing in front of her, catching her shoulders.

She jumped.

And he remembered the shit she'd been through—the shit he knew about, anyway—and what he was coming to realize was just some small portion of the hell she'd endured.

"Shit, Peaches," he muttered, immediately dropping his hands and taking a step back. "I'm so sorry. I-I know you don't like to be touched."

She stilled and that head tilted to the side.

Eyes studying him as though she could see into his soul. "But..." She trailed off, shook her head.

"What?" he asked, digging his toes into the soles of his shoes, stopping himself from stepping forward, stopping himself from taking her into his arms.

"You don't like me."

He was the one to inhale now, a sharp puff of air nearly choking him up.

Or maybe that was the remorse. The regret.

A-fucking-gain.

"Mads—"

"Don't lie," she said quickly.

"It's not that I don't like you," he began.

"Okay," she said, her tone going sad. "It's that you hate me for what I put Ben through." A sigh that hurt his heart. "Don't worry. I hate myself too."

"Don't," he rasped.

And yeah, it was a fucking *rasp*. Because she was killing him, and he'd contributed to that, and—

"I am so sorry," he said. "I did this. *This* is my fault and—"

"Me doing drugs is your fault?" she asked softly. "Me being raped by my stepfather and numbing my mind in any way possible is *your* fault? Me losing years because I was chasing that blank emptiness because I couldn't stand being in my own head is *your* fault?"

Pain ricocheted up his arms and it took him a second to realize it was because he was clenching his hands into fists so tightly that his bones were protesting. What he knew about all she'd endured? He knew nothing. Fucking *nothing*. "That's not your fault either—"

Her mouth curved up into a half smile. "*I'm* the one who took the drugs, who drank myself into oblivion. Who hurt the people around me because I was torn to shreds inside."

His fists clenched tighter, more pain up his arms. And yet, that couldn't compare to the pain in his heart. "Mads. Christ. *Fuck*."

"What?" she asked, still soft.

"I wish that hadn't happened to you."

Her smile faded and she shrugged. "You can't change the past. You can only move forward."

"It's what you do with the second and third and fourth chances?"

That smile came back at her words from the previous night. It was small and faint. But it was there.

And seeing it was almost as good as winning the Cup.

"I wish I could hug you right now," he blurted.

Her head did that tilting thing again. "Why can't you hug me?"

"You don't like to be touched."

Her mouth opened, closed. "That's twice you've said that now," she said, but quietly, almost like it was to herself, and before he could respond, explain why he'd come to that conclusion, she went on, "I don't like to be touched when I can't see it coming. Like when you startled me back at the...well, you know," she added with a wave of her hand. "When I'm comfortable with someone, when I see the contact coming, I'm okay." She nibbled on her bottom lip. "I'm actually better than okay with it, especially when someone gives good hug."

His heart began beating faster.

"And you know what I've learned?" she asked.

He shook his head. "No, Peaches, I don't know what you've learned."

She stepped closer, the toes of her shoes bumping against his. "I've learned that hockey players give *great* hugs."

His pulse was thundering in his veins, in his ears, but he managed to lift a hand.

Slowly, so *fucking* slowly, he raised it.

Up, up, *up*.

Stroking his fingertips lightly along her jaw, just beneath the bruise on her cheek.

A bruise he fucking hated.

But when she didn't flinch, when her eyes slid closed and her body hitched the slightest bit forward, he allowed himself to shift.

Sliding his hand back, dipping it into the silken strands of her hair. Wrapping his other arm around her, drawing her into him.

Hugging her.

Tightly.

For a long time.

Whispering "I'm sorry" when the apology wouldn't stay lodged in his throat any longer.

Her arms tightened around him.

Then loosened, and he listened to the nonverbal cue, dropping his arms, stepping back, hating the space that had come between them.

Her fingers wrapped around his. "I know," she whispered back.

Then she walked away.

His eyes went back to that center rink, back to the memories and nostalgia and—

"Lucas?"

He whipped around. "Yeah?"

"For the record, you give great hug."

FIFTEEN

MADS

She'd gone in to work because what else did she have to do? But even being with her kids didn't make her feel better.

Because they'd all noticed the bruise and every response on the scale of reactions felt shitty. There was outrage (from her boss, Margie, and many of the kids) and worry for her (the majority of the kids fell into this category) and worse, there was the quiet, the solemn eyes noticing the bruise for exactly it was, knowing because they'd experienced it (only a few of the kids responded like this).

Mads shouldn't have come.

Not until the bruise had faded.

Or she'd found some super-duper powerful concealer to make it seem like it wasn't there.

The quiet was the worst.

Absolutely.

Because she'd lived *that* quiet.

But most concerning was Vivi's response.

She'd gone silent and solemn *and* the guilt on her face—

"Enough," Mads whispered and deliberately shoved that thought from her mind.

She'd find a time to talk to Vivi, and it would all be okay.

It *had* to be.

Unfortunately, she knew all too well that positive thoughts and hoping things would turn out all right was bullshit.

Fate liked to be a real bitch.

Things went wrong, people got hurt, and—

"*Enough,*" she muttered, grunting as she lifted a box, stretching up and rising onto her tiptoes so that she could shove it on the top shelf. After the breadth of responses, she'd relegated herself to the storage room and the long overdue task of reorganizing the supplies here—seeing what needed to be tossed, what they needed to order, what goodies she could pull out for the kids.

At least here she wasn't doing any damage to her kids.

She continued her process of open, sort, lift out of the way, doing it for long enough that her ibuprofen wore off and her head started pounding, and sadly enough, her entire body began to ache. She needed to add some weight training into her exercise routine.

Which meant that her exercise routine would consist of... weight training.

Chuckling to herself, she reached for the last box just as there was a knock on the door. "Come in!" she called, tugging the cardboard flaps open, seeing that the random mishmash of items inside was going to require more time than she had left that day to sort through and pushing it aside.

Margie swept into the room, expression placid, but her eyes went thunderous when they hit on Mads's face.

Cool as a cucumber, except for the couple of tells.

"I'm fine," Mads reminded her.

"I'm walking you to your car tonight," Margie ordered, crossing her arms and clearly not going to take any lip about the proclamation. "And going forward, you will not dismiss security early because you feel bad about them staying late." She narrowed her eyes, daring Mads to disagree.

Considering the bruise marring half her face, she wasn't going to. "Okay."

More narrowing. Then a nod toward the box. "Leave that for another day. It's time to close up."

"I"—she'd just put it away and—

That brow furrowed further, Margie's gaze burning into her.

"Right," she said, pushing up, brushing her hands on the fronts of her jeans. "It's time to close up," she repeated with a nod.

Margie's glare remained in place, but the thunder in her eyes cleared slightly. "I'll meet you in my office."

"Okay."

A huff and she started to turn away.

But then she whipped around so quickly that Mads rocked back on her heels.

"I'm so sorry you weren't safe here," she said, hand lifting. She squeezed Mads's arm, the regret so heavy in her tone that it was an almost palpable presence in the room. "I'll make sure that never happens again."

"It's not your—"

But by then Margie had dropped her hand, was already spinning around, hustling out of the storage room.

Guilt. Remorse.

Too fucking much of it going around.

Lucas. Ben. Margie. *Her.*

That had her pausing halfway toward bending for the box, intending to shove it back into a corner where it would probably languish for several more months before she found the gumption to go back to sorting.

She straightened, leaving the box, forgetting about putting organizing off for months.

Because—*God*—she wasn't the only one with the past eating at her. Everyone in her life, everyone around her, was filled with some amount of remorse, of guilt, and she was tired of it.

Why were they punishing themselves over and over again?

Why were they content to just sit in that whirlwind of hurts, allowing themselves to be beaten up over and over again?

Why was *she*?

Not just the bruises and physical hurts, but all the rest of it.

"Fuck," she whispered, eyes welling, legs shaking, hand gripping at the edge of the shelf because...*she. Was. Done.*

With regret.

With self-reproach.

With being the biggest and most intensely negative presence in her own life.

Trauma—it was fucking brutal enough without her adding her own bricks to the top of the pile, weighing herself down even further.

Her hand tightened almost to the point of pain. Her breathing sped. Her forehead settled against the shelving's metal frame.

But that feeling inside her didn't change, even as she slowly regained control of herself, mind spinning through Lucas and Ben, Margie and Lily. Through *her* own brain with all those sharp, dangerous edges.

So many Band-Aids, bandages hastily slapped into place.

Covering up the bleeding.

But not stopping it.

Not *ever* stopping it.

No wonder she was exhausted. She was constantly bleeding out.

And instead of trying to heal herself, she was making a thousand more cuts.

The question was...how did she stop?

"Ready?" Margie called from down the hall, impatience in her tone, leaving Mads with a realization but no solution to that internal discovery.

No solution except for...time.

And the fortitude to continue moving forward.

———

"This is dumb," she whispered almost a week later, the cold of night biting at her skin through the thin material of her jacket.

Her bruise was almost gone—or at least easily coverable with her standard-issue concealer.

There had been no sign of Nick, and security or Margie escorted her to her car every night since the attack. There had also been no sign of a certain hockey player—minus the fresh lock that she saw every time she went in and out of her apartment.

But worryingly, there had also been no sign of Vivi.

For the last week, Olivia had not returned to the youth center, and though Mads had looked for her during every drive home, she hadn't seen her walking the streets either.

"That's a good thing," she whispered. "She's with her dad and safe and—"

It was also what had driven her to cross boundaries.

"It's just to make sure she's okay," she whispered, checking her watch, seeing that she had a few more minutes left until she needed to leave to meet up with Marcus and Sam.

Suitably shored up, she hitched her purse onto her shoulder, popped the driver's side door, and hurried up to the house where she'd dropped Vivi off that night a couple of weeks ago. It was a smaller home with a slightly shabby paint job, but the planters held blooming flowers and there were toys on the front lawn, a bike propped against a wooden pillar. A ribbon-adorned wreath hung from the front door.

It was a *home*.

Her nerves settled. This was what Vivi needed.

She walked up the steps that led to that door, brows dragging together when she caught sight of the doormat, those nerves immediately ramping up again.

The Fosters.

Foster being...*not* Vivi's last name.

Mads lifted a hand to press the doorbell but the knob turned, the wooden panel flying open. "Oh," the woman who Mads would have assumed was Vivi's dad's girlfriend, if not for the pieces starting to slide into place in her mind, said, staggering back a step, her hand pressed to her chest.

"I'm sorry," Mads said. "I didn't mean to startle you. I was just looking for Vivi—Olivia," she added quickly when the woman frowned.

"Olivia?"

More pieces moving into position. Mads's stomach beginning to twist. "Yeah," she said. "Olivia Wright. She lives here, right?"

"Olivia," the woman said softly, brows still furrowed. "Oh. *Olivia.*"

Her head tilted to the side.

"But she doesn't live here."

SIXTEEN

LUCAS

He was late.

Fuck, he hated being late.

Especially when it was a situation like this—a team bonding event with all the back and front office staff and the players and everyone's families.

And he was the asshole rolling up ten minutes after it had started.

"Christ," he muttered, throwing his car into park and reaching into the back to snag his skates. Then he hustled his ass into the rink.

The smell and nostalgia hit him, just like it did every time he strode through the lobby.

But this time he wasn't able to enjoy it.

Because he was late.

For fuck's sake.

"Lucas!"

He blinked, tabled his annoyance—he was only irritated at himself, anyway—and turned toward the voice, already knowing it was going to belong to an adorable tiny creature.

And yeah, he'd keep the *creature* thoughts to himself, especially when it came to children.

"Hi, buddy," he said to the little human who was decked out in minature hockey gear that had the kiddo resembling more of a marshmallow than an actual athlete.

"I'm playing hockey today!" the boy cried, jumping up and down on his skates and promptly losing his balance.

Before he could topple completely to the ground, Lucas reached out and caught him. "Whoa, there."

"I'm a hockey player," the boy said. "I'm tough."

"I know you are." Lucas righted him. "But it's okay to not be tough sometimes."

The little boy tilted his head to the side, studying Lucas as though he'd just imparted state secrets. "Okay," he whispered.

Lucas smiled, lifted his fist for a bump. "Now go play hockey, bud."

A nod that nearly sent his little body tumbling again.

Then he was teetering and he ran across the lobby, falling down and getting up several times along the way but not stopping as he headed for the open door to the center rink.

"That was really sweet of you."

He looked up into the eyes of the reason he'd kept the *creature* thoughts in his mind.

He loved kids.

He wanted some of his own, if he ever got to the point where he thought he might be a good father.

But they were still tiny, confusing creatures that came with tears and snot and chaos.

"He seems like a cool little boy." Lucas smiled, but inched back a step. Because just as he understood that kids came with all that snot and tantrums and chaos, he knew very well what the gleam in the mom's eyes meant.

A flick down to her left hand showed a narrow band of white skin.

Newly divorced.

Or widowed.

But that gleam told him she was freshly divorced.

And, look, she was a beautiful woman. Gorgeous in just a simple pair of jeans, minimal makeup, and her hair tied back into a ponytail.

It was just...he didn't shit where he ate.

Okay, that was a lie.

The truth was that his dick was broken—or fixated on the one woman he couldn't allow himself to want. He wasn't into the asshole routine (despite recent demonstrations of his asshole abilities), and he didn't believe in the whole dark, damaged hero redeeming himself bullshit.

He'd fucked up. Too many times.

Mads deserved better, even if she *might* give him a second chance.

But that didn't mean he was going to...

What?

It didn't mean that he wasn't going to take it?

Another fucking lie.

Because if Mads gave him that smallest opening, he'd be in there and—

No.

God. Fuck.

What the fuck was wrong with him?

A hand on his arm and he tensed. Shit, he was late and his mind was a fucking mess and he'd forgotten there was a predator in front of him.

Those fingers tightened, and his eyes flew open, his tongue already forming the gentle but definitive rebuttal. Only when he looked into a pair of dark brown eyes, he realized he'd been wrong. Not predatory.

Hiding the kind of bone-deep sadness that made his heart ache.

Her mouth curved, just slightly. "If he or she makes you think that hard, then I think you already have your answer."

"What?" he whispered.

"You've got lovestruck written all over you," she said softly, her fingers squeezing gently. "This is just your push to reach out and take it, okay? Even if your brain comes up with a million reasons why it's a bad idea." The other half of her mouth turned up, completing a smile that was as beautiful as it was sad. "Trust me."

Then she dropped her hand, started to walk away.

"Wait," he said, moving after her. "I—"

"It's okay," she told him when he stalled out on his words. "I know my advice came from left field." She tilted her head. "And I think you were in a hurry before Matteo stopped you. Don't let me keep you."

This is just your push to reach out and take it.

"Her name is Mads," he blurted. "And I fucked up so big that I don't think, morally, I can justify shoving myself into her life."

The woman's shoulders lifted and fell. "Who ever said that love is moral?"

He sucked in a breath so quickly that he nearly choked.

But she was still speaking. "Life goes wrong. People die. Hearts get broken. We mistreat each other. But do we *grow?* Do we try to do better?" She shrugged. "I don't know your Mads, but I do know that if it was *my* heart that needed looking after, I'd want the guy who would work his ass off, who'd kill himself, who'd offer his own heart up in sacrifice in order to protect it." A sigh. "Even *if* he was initially the one to stomp on it."

Lucas blinked. "That shouldn't make sense."

"I know," she whispered. "But somehow, it does."

"Yeah," he whispered back. "It does."

The woman smiled, and it was still sad, still beautiful. "Are you ready to offer your heart up as tribute to her?"

Was he?

There wasn't even any hesitation. The bright, flashing billboard in his mind emblazoned with "Yes! Fucking *yes!*" was answer enough.

Or maybe obvious enough.

Because the sad left the woman's smile. "Yeah," she murmured. "I thought so." A whistle trilled, and she glanced away. "Bye, Lucas." She started toward the rink onto which little Matteo had disappeared, paused, and looked back over her shoulder. "Thanks for telling him what you did." Her throat worked. "Sometimes I think he worries too much about—" A shake of her head. "Anyway, he just...it was good for him to hear those words from his favorite player."

"You're welcome..." he began, then realized he didn't know her name.

"Lauren," she said, proving once again that he was either an open book or she had mind reading abilities.

"Well, Lauren, you and Matteo are welcome to join us on the other Gold's rink after practice if he's not too tired."

"Oh no, we couldn't."

"We're just having a skating event, and he'd be right at home with the other hooligans."

"We can't impose—"

Lucas glanced at the rink, his gut telling him that this woman needed the family that was the Gold even more than he did. "Might tire him out." A nod toward Matteo skating around like a madman.

She sighed. "I'll believe that when I see it," she said. "That kid never runs out of energy."

"Lauren?"

Her eyes flicked back to his. "Yeah?" she asked softly.

"You gave me some solid advice"—with a side of ESP, but that wasn't the point, and anyway, his own brand of psychic abilities was pinging—"so maybe you'll be open to accepting some?"

Her nose wrinkled and it was fucking cute.

Not for him.

But fucking cute.

"It's easier to give advice than accept it," she pointed out, quite rightly—and still cute.

He wasn't going to let this go, though.

"When a Gold player invites you into the fold, you accept the summons."

"Why does that sound like the mafia?"

He snorted. "Maybe because sometimes it kind of is?"

"And that's supposed to make me feel better?"

"No," he admitted, mouth curving. "But I can promise you will if you join in on the fun."

Her mouth opened, but no protest came out. She just shook her head, smiled, and nodded at the Gold's practice rink. "I think you were late when you were coming in."

"Deflection." But he gave her that move, made one of his own. "See you both in a bit."

"I—"

Then he walked away and did it in a hurry. Because as she pointed out, he was late.

And so was she when she and Matteo eventually made their way onto the practice rink.

Just call him the Fog City Medium.

Seventeen

Mads

She glared at her brother. "You didn't mention the skating."

Ben grinned up at her, totally unperturbed as he tied her skates like the baby she was. "I figured that the event being held at the ice rink was indication enough."

Marcus and Sam had gotten their own skates on, just needing a little tightening from her brother.

Mads, on the other hand, was a hopeless case.

She'd knotted the laces, nearly disemboweled herself when she'd tripped trying to return to the bench, and now was sitting on the cold metal seat like a child while her brother did up her skates.

Ben did another tighten, nearly yanking her off the bench then secured the laces with a knot.

Then he went to work on the other one. "So, are you going to tell me what's bothering you?"

His tone was casual, but there was worry there, sitting right under the surface.

"It's not about Nick," she told him. "I haven't seen him since that night, and I'm still being escorted to my car every night."

She didn't miss the way his shoulders relaxed slightly.

"And the protective order was filed and approved by the judge."

That had him relaxing further, making dealing with the police worth it. Anything that might bring her brother some peace of mind was worth it.

She'd done as she'd promised Lucas, had told Ben about Nick. First, because she wasn't a liar any longer. Second, because after she'd confronted him about the lock, she'd gone back out to her car and found Ben there.

No avoiding her brother.

No hiding the bruise.

So...he knew the truth and that was why she knew he was watching out for her more closely than normal.

It was why she was here.

And not only just because her nephews were cute as fuck and could get her to do pretty much anything, but because her brother had been worried and she'd needed to give him that play.

So, she was here.

Skating.

Heaven help her.

"And I'm worried about one of my kids," Mads admitted. "She freaked when she realized Nick was at the youth center and I got hurt." She took his hand when he held it out. "And now she hasn't come back." And wasn't staying where she'd told Mads she was staying.

Something she didn't mention, even though that had been eating at her for the last week.

The woman—the mom of one of Vivi's old elementary school friends (which had explained why Vivi's name hadn't ring a bell), hadn't seen Vivi in years apparently.

Even though Mads had watched her retrieve the hide-a-key and walk through the front door.

Something she also hadn't mentioned.

Because either Mads and her old friend were closer than the mom knew, or she'd watched Vivi commit a crime and she wasn't going to throw her charge under the bus without understanding exactly what the fuck was going on.

Something that would be a hell of a lot easier if Vivi just reappeared.

Unfortunately, Mads knew very well that disappearing was a skill and if Vivi didn't want to be found, she wouldn't be.

"You haven't seen her at all?" Ben asked, tugging her up to her feet.

Mads shook her head. "She hasn't been back to the center since the day after Nick assaulted me in the parking lot."

Another person who excelled at disappearing.

And who she hoped to God hadn't disappeared *with* Vivi.

"Damn." Ben's expression filled with concern. "Should we go out and look for her?" He hitched a thumb. "I can round up some of the guys—"

"No," she said, heart squeezing because, goddamn, but she loved her brother. "That will just scare her. It was hard to get her to trust me, and if I push it, she might never come back."

His concern didn't fade, but he nodded, wrapping an arm around her shoulders. "That changes, you let me know."

"I will."

A glance at her. "Promise."

She poked his belly with her finger. "Don't push it, big bro." A beat. "But I promise."

Of course she did.

Because it was Ben and he loved her, and she knew how lucky she was to have him in her life and because...Vivi might need him *and* the Gold cavalry.

"Damn right, you do."

She narrowed her eyes at him. "Watch it."

"I'm not scared of you," he said lightly, thankfully taking her cue and continuing to nudge the conversation towards easier topics. "You're Bambi."

She *was* wobbling on her skates.

Pathetically.

One would think that she would have picked up some sort of skating ability, what with having an NHL player for a brother.

Alas, she *was* Bambi.

And she hadn't even stepped foot on the ice yet.

"Dad!"

Her heart squeezed when Sam came in hot, running on his skates like they'd been surgically attached to his feet—and with absolutely no wobble in sight.

Hearing the moniker in relation to her brother had been strange at first—the kids had a dad...only their bio dad was a piece of shit and her brother had been more of a solid, caring, *permanent* figure in their lives than their sperm donor ever had.

That was why *Dad* fit.

Why she loved it for him.

Sam didn't stop, crashing into her brother and wrapping his arms around Ben's middle from behind, rocking him forward slightly upon impact. But Ben didn't lose his balance and end up on the black skate mat like she would have. He just tugged Sam around to his side and kept him there in a side hug.

That again sent her heart squeezing.

Because that too was why *Dad* fit.

"Hi, Aunt Mads." Sam bounced slightly. "I can't believe you came. Dad says you hate skating."

"And miss out on spending time with you?" she told him. "Plus, skating isn't *all* that bad."

Ben snorted.

She glared.

Sam started bouncing again, clearly ready to get out there.

"What's up, bud?" Ben asked gently.

"Are you ready?"

Impatient. Yup.

Just like his dad.

"Almost," Ben told him, slanting her a grin, his tone filled with the patience that only came from being a parent, biological, adopted, or otherwise.

Watching him interact with the boys always filled her insides with cotton candy—sticky, sweet, evaporating in an instant but leaving the pleasing aftertaste on her tongue for ages.

Silly, she knew.

But the description made sense in her own mind.

And she'd take that pleasant, lingering sweetness any day of the week.

"When are we going to skate?" Sam asked, releasing the hug. "Everyone is already out there!"

Ben nodded. "I'm just going to help your aunt—"

Sam's face fell.

He knew exactly how well-developed her skating skills were... and how long it would take for her to get out there.

"Go," Mads told them. "You know it's going to take me ten years to get to the ice. You can both do some laps and still meet me by the door to save Bambi from broken bones."

Sam's head tilted to the side, excited again at the prospect of skating. "Who's Bambi?"

She widened her eyes. "A fictional deer from a classic children's movie your dad *should* have shown you."

Ben shuddered, shaking his head in a way that had her mouth curving up. "I'd like to avoid the traumatizing, thank you very much."

That was a good point.

Something she opened her mouth up to tell him—

"Why's it traumatizing?" Sam asked.

Ben shot her a look—a very disappointed, Dad-like look. "Thanks," he muttered. "You know he's not going to let it go now."

"Let what—" Sam asked, brows furrowing.

"Oh, look!" she cried, going for diversion because her brother really *did* have a point. "Marcus is already out there."

"What?" Sam whipped around, saw his brother on the ice and started hightailing it for the door. "Hurry up, Dad!" He paused before hopping on the ice. "Thanks, Aunt Mads!"

Ben sighed and shook his head, mouth tipping up. "Nice save, auntie."

"I try," she told him softly.

"I know." A tug of her hair. "Move slow and bend your knees, yeah?"

She nodded.

Something he'd told her a thousand times.

Something she always promptly forgot the moment she got up on these torture devices.

"I've got it. Now go," she ordered. "Your boys want you."

He kissed the top of her head. "They want you too." He released her. "And we all *need* you too."

Something she was starting to realize as the guilt and past continued to recede.

Something that meant she still had that lingering sweetness on her taste buds as she shuffled to the rink, lifted a foot.

Placed it onto the ice.

Pushed forward...

And promptly went full Bambi.

Eighteen

Lucas

"Ouch," Rome muttered from next to him.

"What?" Lucas asked, glancing up at his teammate and seeing Rome was staring out at the ice. He was almost laced up—still late and made later by the interaction with Matteo and Lauren.

He made a mental note of the time, was going to send in the troops if necessary to get that little firecracker out here, and Lauren into the fold. If only because his gut told him that she needed some nice people in her life.

Considering how often his gut had betrayed him of late, maybe that was the wrong call.

Or maybe, he was finally *listening* to his instincts, not reacting out of fear and rage and shitty memories.

Because when he glanced up, his stomach did a flip.

Mads was sitting on the ice, head thrown back in laughter, gorgeous hair shining as it flowed in deep brown locks down her spine. Her light jeans were stained dark at the knees and covered in snow, so that clearly was not the first time she'd ended up on the ice that day.

"Why isn't anyone helping her?" he muttered, bending again, fingers working at the laces.

"We've all been taking turns," Rome said. "I've never seen a more hopeless, clumsy skater." He shook his head, chuckling. "And to think that Ben is so fucking smooth on the ice. Where did the hockey genetics go?"

Lucas glared at his teammate, not liking the fact that Mads had clearly fallen more than once, and definitely not liking that Rome was making fun of her. "I'm sure she's fine—"

He hissed out a breath.

Because Sam and Marcus had drawn her up to her skates...

And she'd lasted all of one stride.

Because she'd ended up on her ass again, this time taking Sam and Marcus down with her.

Jesus.

The woman was going to break a bone.

Or twenty.

Sam and Marcus clambered up like the hockey players they were, and they reached out like they were going to help Mads up again—like the good people they were—but Lucas knew that shit was going to go as well as what had landed Mads on the ice several times over already.

He finished with his lace, popped up to his feet.

"Where are you—?"

But he didn't bother to listen to the rest of Rome's question, certainly didn't hang around to answer it. Not when Mads was out there.

Falling down.

Again and again.

Are you ready to offer your heart up as tribute to her?

He stepped onto the ice.

Lauren's question from earlier was a fucking terrifying notion...until he saw Mads fall again, knew he wasn't going to be there in time to catch her.

Knew that the only thing scarier would be *not* trusting his heart to her safekeeping.

It's what you do with those chances that really shows who you are inside.

Fuck, Mads was smart and generous and way too forgiving.

And that was why he knew it was time for him to stop fucking around.

To stop hiding from his future, from what he wanted.

Her laughter reached his ears first—light and sweet and *his*. He wanted to hoard it like a fucking dragon, to collect it like the treasure it was and never let it out of his sight.

Then he was at her side, kneeling next to her. "Mads."

Her laughter cut off, replaced by a wary sort of chuckle, as though she were waiting on him to be a dick to her again.

Never again.

Never fucking again.

But then the wariness cleared and she smiled at him. "Fancy meeting you here," she said lightly.

"Whatcha doing down there?" he asked, continuing with that light.

Because her smile...well, it was carving his heart out, all on its own. He just had to place it on the silver platter.

"Oh, you know," she said, mouth curved, "I'm just inspecting the quality of the ice. Have to make sure it's safe for all of you guys."

He grinned. "Yeah? You're just looking after us, then?"

"Exactly."

He extended a hand. "Want to do that inspecting from up here?"

She brushed her palms on her jeans. "You sure you can handle me?"

That had his heart squeezing. "Yeah, Peaches, I am."

Her ponytail bounced as she tilted her head, smile fading. No doubt taking in the seriousness of his tone. "I—"

"Aunt Mads! Dad says he'll come and help you up," Sam

announced, skating over to them at speed...and stopping abruptly, showering them with snow.

"Easy, buddy," Lucas told him, nudging him back since Mads's hands were on the ice, too close for his comfort to her nephew's skates. "You can tell your dad I've got her."

Mads startled.

Probably recognizing his declaration would stir up drama in the locker room and send Ben's protective instincts flaring...and maybe a fist flying in Lucas's direction.

But Lucas was finally getting his head out of his ass, and he wasn't going to hide it. Wasn't going to hide the way he felt about Mads, nor all the ways he was going to make it up to her.

Plus, Ben had married Josh—their captain's—sister.

He had no room to talk.

"But she's Bambi!"

Lucas blinked, glanced back over at Mads.

Who giggled and waved her nephew away. "I think Lucas is strong enough to help me. Go enjoy time with your dad, yeah?"

A shrug. "Okay!"

Then Sam was zooming off, flying around the ice like he'd been born to it, not that he'd just begun learning how to skate when they'd moved to California a couple of years ago.

Mads giggled again. "How is he a better skater than me?"

"I don't know," Lucas said baldly, earning another giggle.

"Rude."

"No," he said. "But I have been."

She sucked in a breath.

"No more, though," he promised.

Her breath hissed out. "Lucas..."

"No more."

"I told you it's fine—"

Yeah, it wasn't. But as she'd told him in that car ride weeks before, it was what people did with the second—or third or fourth—chances they were given. So...no more indecision. No more being an asshole. No more hiding the real reason he'd lashed out so violently. He'd level with her. Explain. Make good on that second—or twentieth—chance.

But not right now.

Not right here.

Right in this moment, he wanted her safely on her feet, enjoying herself, her fingers not at risk of amputation. "How's that gorgeous behind of yours feeling?"

She blinked, ponytail waving when her head tilted to the side, cheeks going pink as she studied him for a long moment before admitting, "Cold."

"Want me to help you with that?"

Her lips twitched. "There are children present."

"Scamp," he teased, then shifted behind her, wrapping his arms around her middle. "This okay?" he asked, a moment too late.

He'd need to be more aware, to make sure she knew the contact was coming before he actually touched her—

"It's fine."

"It's—"

One of her hands closed over his. "I promise it's *fine*."

He shook his head. "I—"

"My butt's still cold, by the way," she said, leaning back into him, her fingers surrounding his squeezing lightly.

"I—" He lost his head of steam. Mostly because when she'd leaned into him, her body had pressed back against his and she'd drawn him closer, bringing his arms further around her. Flowers in his nose. Curves all along his front. His pulse sped, cock stirring, and he knew that he needed to move or else he was really going to give Ben a reason to introduce his face to his friend's fist. "One, two, *three!*"

She squeaked when he moved at speed, popping her up to her skates, banding his arm even tighter around her when her feet immediately slid out from beneath her. "Did they even give you a sharpened pair?"

A glare up at him, one that nearly sent her toppling again.

"Funny," she muttered, clinging to his arm around her middle, pressing against him even more firmly.

Not helping the whole situation south of his border.

"I now understand the Bambi reference," he said dryly.

"Still not funny," she muttered, feet *sort of* steady underneath her.

"You ready to move forward?"

She looked up at him so quickly that he nearly lost his balance.

Thankfully, he was a fucking professional hockey player. He could keep his feet. Even when she was looking at him like *that*.

Like she'd just slotted the final puzzle piece into place.

"I thought you didn't like me," she whispered, the words barely reaching his ears.

"No," he whispered back. "No, I don't feel that way at all."

She lifted her hand, touched his jaw. "Yeah. I'm starting to see that." Then she stretched further, arching against him so she could press her lips to his cheek. A breath. "I'm ready to move forward."

And she *did* move forward.

Only this time, he wasn't ready.

He was fixated on that gentle brush of her mouth on his skin.

She wobbled, jerking hard against his hold.

And...

He ended up breaking her fall.

So maybe it was less his heart on a silver platter and more his ass being served up to this woman.

Funnily enough, he found that he didn't care either way.

Nineteen

Mads

"How are we doing in here?" Margie asked.

And then promptly stopped dead.

Probably because they—or Mads, anyway—wasn't doing well in there, not at all. They'd had another movie night and the space...showed it.

Popcorn littered the carpet, whole kernels to crumbled bits. Candy wrappers overflowed the trash bins and she could see the sticky fingerprints on the tabletops. Empty bottles and napkins and half-filled paper cups were dotted on top of each and every one of the flat surfaces.

Many of the kids had offered to stay and clean up.

But she'd told them to go home.

Because it was late and this was her job.

Even if this was something that would have sent her scrambling, maybe even for a bottle of wine, for a hit of something, just to ease the tension, erase the panic that was beginning to creep into her mind, making her worry that she'd never get this room back into order.

And if she didn't—

She pressed her tongue to the roof of her mouth, inhaled, slow and steady, through her nose.

There was no one to yell at her, no one to hit her, no one to punish her by creeping into her bedroom in the dead of night and using and abusing her body.

"Mads?"

She exhaled, slow and steady as on the way in, using the techniques she'd learned in therapy to calm her pulse, to settle her stomach and heart.

If she didn't finish cleaning, it would hold until tomorrow.

And that would be okay.

Margie had moved closer, lightly touched her arm. "Mads," she said softly.

"Sorry." Another breath, this one short and staccato, shoving away the urge to numb, the panic, the past. "I was having an existential crisis about popcorn. Don't mind me."

"I'll stay and help clean up."

"What?" Mads said, gently pushing her boss toward the door. "No, you won't! Brian"—Margie's husband who she barely saw because he traveled for work and Margie put in enough hours here at the center for three people—"is taking you on your first date in forever. And"—a glance at her watch—"if you don't leave right now, you'll be late for the movie."

Indecision on Margie's face.

"I'm fine," she pushed. "I promise. I'll lock up after you."

"And make sure security walks you out to your car?"

Mads nodded. "Yes."

More indecision on her boss's face, and so before Margie could talk herself out of leaving, Mads took her arm, which already had her purse hanging from it—see? her boss *needed* to go —and started tugging her toward the front door.

Reaching for it at the same time there was a knock on the other side of it.

She and Margie looked at each other.

But then the door was opening, Pascal, the head of their security company, popping his head in. "Ladies," he said, appearing completely unsurprised, even though they were both standing just a couple of inches from the threshold. His gaze slid to Mads's. "You have a visitor."

"Oh, I—"

Her heart squeezed. Was it Vivi?

Only then Pascal was tugging the door a little wider and it wasn't a slender teenage girl standing on the other side.

It was Lucas.

"Oh," she breathed, then felt her cheeks flare because that sounded rude.

And disappointed.

And *rude.*

Especially after she'd all but crushed the man on the ice the day before. Only once, but considering that she could barely sit in a chair without her butt protesting, she didn't think his butt was faring much better.

"I—"

He grinned, eyes dancing. "Usually you save the disappointed sigh for when you call me Lucifer."

Mads's cheeks went hotter. "I'm sorry. I just thought that my visitor might be Vivi."

His amusement faded. "Still no sign of her?"

She shook her head. "No."

"Damn," he muttered. "Is there anything that I can do to help find her?"

Mads sighed. "No. I've driven around a bit, trying to spot her, but if she doesn't want to be found, she's not going to be found."

"I can find her."

Mads blinked, tearing her gaze from Lucas's, realizing that they weren't alone for the first time in several minutes.

And...her cheeks had to be fire engine red by now.

She glanced at Pascal. "She's really good at hiding."

A corner of Pascal's mouth turned up. "I'm really good at finding people."

"He is," Margie and Lucas both said at the same time, setting Mads blinking again, only this time her gaze was shifting between her boss and her...well, her hockey player, she supposed. He wasn't *hers*, but she—

Whatever, she was just going with it for the moment.

Because she had bigger fish to fry.

First, Margie—because Mads was blushing enough already without deep diving into her emotions about Lucas.

She lifted her brows in question.

Her boss just shrugged, hitched her purse a little higher, and leaned in to gently squeeze her. "Why do you think we hired him?" She leaned back, smiled, adding softly, "Have fun with your hockey player."

Your hockey player.

Her hockey player.

That was a thought pulled by Margie straight from the recesses of Mads's mind.

It was a thought that was...entirely too easy to accept.

"I—"

"Come on, Pascal," Margie said. "Walk me to my car, and I'll tell you about our Vivi."

Pascal, man of few words that he was, just nodded and followed her out, but not before he looked at Mads, waited for her to nod, to silently tell him she was okay with him leaving her here with Lucas.

And God, he was such a good guy.

She smiled, sent him another nod when he lifted a brow. He nodded back then flicked a narrow-eyed glare at Lucas, warning him nonverbally.

"I won't leave her alone," Lucas said softly.

"See that you don't," Margie called from outside the center.

Pascal nodded one more time, pausing only to make sure the

door shut, calling through the small, reinforced pane of glass above the knob, "Lock up."

Lucas reached forward and flicked the lock.

Then turned back toward her.

And suddenly she was all sorts of awkward, especially when he was standing there with gentle eyes, mouth half hitched up, and stubble dotting his cheeks. "I—um—" She was grasping at conversational straws because the awkward had crawled up her throat and coated the back of her tongue. "How do you know Pascal?"

There.

That was brilliant.

Or coherent anyway.

"His company does security for the team."

Oh. Right.

Maybe she should have known that? Ben had mentioned a security company after Nick and—

"Mads?"

She swallowed, awkward making a reappearance. "Yeah?"

"What else do you need to do before you can head home?"

She winced.

He rocked back on his heels. "That much?"

"Well," she hedged. "It doesn't all have to be done tonight." A shrug. "I can finish up tomorrow."

He studied her closely. "Except that will bug you all night, won't it?"

Another wince. "Probably."

"I'm here. I'll help."

"Why?"

His brows drew together. "Why will I help you?"

Great, she'd already been rude about him showing up and now she was making it seem like he was the kind of person who didn't help out. When she knew it was the opposite. He was very generous with his time, both to the team and his friends.

She just...hadn't been part of either one of those before.

"No," she said quickly. "I...uh...was just wondering why you were here in the first place. You know," she blabbered on, "you seem to be coming to the center a lot and—"

"Mads?"

She pressed her lips together, released them. "Yeah?"

"I'm here because *you're* here."

TWENTY

LUCAS

His words stunned her.

He saw it in the way she faltered, in the shaking hand pushing back the wisps of hair that had escaped her ponytail. "Oh," she whispered.

"Mads?" he asked.

A slow blink. "Yeah?"

"Want to show me what you need to do before you can leave?"

"Oh," she said again. "Right. I just need to clean up after our movie night."

But she didn't move.

"And where was that held, Peaches?"

He'd been here often enough to know most of the space, and he guessed he could just start opening doors.

It'd be faster, though, if she just told him where to start.

She cleared her throat, seemed to shake herself. "That would be helpful, huh?" She relaxed slightly, mouth curving as she started walking down the hall. "It's only one room, but it's a big room," she told him, walking down the hall, reaching for the handle on one of the doors. "And it's also a really big mess."

She pushed the door open.

He froze. "Holy shit."

"Yeah," she said softly. "The kids had...a bit of fun tonight."

He stepped forward into the room, glanced back at her with wide eyes. "Did any of the popcorn even make it into their mouths?"

Mads made a face as she walked in, gaze sweeping the room before coming back to his. "That's my fault. We started booing and throwing popcorn at the bad parts. They"—she swept a hand around—"had much fun with it."

"Was the movie that bad?"

She giggled. "No. It was actually really good. But they really liked throwing the popcorn." A shrug. "And most of the kids offered to stay and clean up. I told them no because they're kids and they have too much on their shoulders anyways. So, tonight is about them being silly and making a mess and not having any responsibilities, even if that's just for a couple of hours before they go home to situations that may not be great."

Jesus. This woman was a fucking saint.

"That's amazing," he murmured, turning toward her, lifting a hand and doing it slowly, incrementally, until he tucked the strand of hair behind her ear that was curled around her cheek, tickling the corner of her mouth if the way she kept pursing her mouth and blowing out air was any indication. "*You're* amazing," he said, rolling that strand of hair between thumb and forefinger. It was like silk, beyond soft.

She pfted. "I'm just a girl who's trying to be better."

He knew that now.

That was why she was so fucking amazing.

And for some reason, he needed her to know it immediately. He bent slightly so their faces were aligned, so she'd see how sincere he was when he said, "I'm in awe of you."

Her face went slack. Then her throat worked. "That doesn't make sense," she whispered.

"What you do is incredible. The person I'm learning you are is beautiful." He dared lower his hand enough to stroke a fingertip across her collarbone. "Inside"—a tap—"and outside."

She sucked in a breath, shook her head. Then blew out the exhale. "It's nothing. Really. They just don't get to be kids a lot. Margie made it so this place is safe for them to be that. All the volunteers—including you and the rest of the Gold organization make that possible—"

"And you," he interjected. "*You* make that possible. I've seen the way they look at you. They know you've been through hell and made it onto the other side." He flattened his palm, felt her pulse thundering beneath the top of her rib cage. "That's why they love you. That's why I'm in awe of you."

Her nostrils flared. "Lucas," she whispered. "You shouldn't say that. You don't know the things I've done."

"I've lived with people who've done the things you've done." Who'd done worse, probably, though he didn't know everything about Mads. Not yet, anyway. "Which is why I know how important it is that these kids have this safe place. And why"—he slid his hand up to her jaw, gently tilting her head back so he held her gaze as he straightened—"I am in absolute awe of you."

Her eyes closed, and she swallowed hard. "I don't know what to say," she murmured.

"You don't have to say anything, Peaches."

Those eyes opened, and his heart convulsed when he saw they were damp, when a tear clung to the bottom lashes.

Shit.

He brushed his thumb along the bottom of her eye, captured that tear. "Don't cry," he practically begged. "I'm not trying to upset you."

He started to pull back, to give her some space or find a tissue or distract her from her tears—

Her hand settled onto his, pressing it back against her cheek. "I'm not upset."

"You're crying."

Her mouth curved. "It's one tear," she admonished lightly, "and it's because I'm touched. Not because I'm upset."

"Oh."

Her smile widened.

Then faded.

And he wondered if it was because of the same thing he'd just realized—

How very close they were standing together.

Only inches separated the fronts of their bodies and, fuck, he wanted to close that small distance so badly, wanted to draw her into his body and to feel her against him, her arms wrapping around his middle, hugging him back—

"You really mean it."

His fingers flexed on her cheek, not needing to ask her what she meant. He could see it in the surprise in her eyes, could see it in the way she held herself so carefully.

Fragile.

But steel beneath.

"Yeah, Peaches, I do."

Her body shifted slightly, the toes of her shoes brushing his, and that minute change in position meant that the next time she inhaled—a deep, long inhale that seemed to come after long moments of not breathing—her breasts brushed against his chest.

Heat exploded in his body, arrowing straight for his groin.

She gasped, fingers tightening over his, and then she paused, seemed to hover on the precipice of a decision.

Now he found that *he* was holding his breath.

Going statue still.

Waiting.

Sensing the next moment would change *everything*.

His heart was in the back of his throat, and his muscles ached from keeping so still and—

She shifted again, and this time it was to move even closer, so that the front of her body was completely flush with his. He lost his battle with control, with holding still, lifting his free hand and settling it on her hip.

Her body jerked, but she didn't pull away.

In fact, she settled even more heavily against him.

Fuck that felt right.

It felt *perfect*.

He dipped his head, halted with his mouth a mere millimeter from hers, inhaling the gasp she released, drinking her in, committing this moment to memory.

Because *this* was one of those times when he knew his life was about to change.

He'd had it when he'd first stepped onto the ice as a kid, this feeling of rightness, of fate, of moving in the direction he was destined for. He'd felt it again when he'd made juniors, when he'd been scouted for college, the night before the draft his sophomore year, and...

He had it now.

Waiting to see if she would close that final bit of distance between them.

Hoping—

She rose on tiptoe and then her lips were against his. Firmly. Not a simple brush and retreat, but as though she'd just fought an inner battle and come out on top.

That was the last thinking he did.

Then it was all sensation, the plumpness of her lips, soft pillows that cushioned his as they kissed, the sleek dart of her tongue when she opened up and allowed him to taste her fully. Breasts and hips that were lush, curves that molded to his body perfectly.

She was perfect.

In the way her free arm wrapped around his shoulders, keeping him close, nails digging lightly into his nape.

One kiss and his cock was hard and aching.

Desperate for more.

But when she pulled back, clinging tightly to his body, his hand, he didn't miss the blip of panic in her eyes before she dropped her head, resting it on his shoulder, puffs of air glazing his skin through his shirt.

He held her, just for a moment more.

Then he dropped his hand from around her waist, slipped the other out from beneath hers, and stepped back. "Okay, Peaches," he said. "We've got quite the mess here. How about you start with the cups and I'll get the vacuum for the popcorn?"

Her head flew up, eyes empty of panic now.

But not empty of emotion.

It was there, blazing and bright, and he knew she felt it too.

Standing on the edge of greatness.

Deciding whether or not to step forward.

Her lips, swollen and reddened from their kiss, pressed flat. Then released.

She exhaled, brushed her fingers against his...and stepped back.

"The vacuum is in the closet in the hall."

Twenty-One

MADS

She'd kissed him.

Kissed Lucas. Lucifer. Asshole number one...

Except he wasn't.

That had been a mask, and he'd removed it—weeks ago now. And tonight he'd given her a glimpse beneath the one he wore beneath *that*, a glimpse into why he'd reacted so virulently to her return to Ben's life.

Protective by nature.

And he'd said he'd lived with people who were like her—

No. Were like how she'd *been*.

She wasn't that person anymore, and she was going to *keep* saying it until that stuck in her brain, until she felt it in her heart, and—

"Want me to toss that, Peaches?" he asked softly.

The vacuum had turned off, something she'd missed considering how in her head she'd been since that kiss. A kiss that had been...

What *had* it been?

Incredible. Absolutely.

Gentle and sweet with a slow burn kind of build. One moment she'd been encased in a fluffy cloud of that saccharine cotton candy and the next it had become...Hot Tamales. Capsules of heat that scorched her taste buds, traveled down her torso, settling in her belly.

Settling...lower.

Which was the moment panic had kicked in.

She was far from a virgin.

But in many ways she felt like one.

Sex had never been her choice, never been something she wanted. At first, it was a violation. Trauma. Hell. Then it had been a tool.

She'd self-pleasured.

A lot, and especially since she'd gotten sober and Jordyn had turned her on to romance novels. The fictional everyone-gets-a-happy-ending books were the perfect bookends to her day...and some of them were so spicy that she'd invested in a really, *really* good vibrator.

So, she was good with self-love.

Some might even say she was a professional.

It was relearning that contact with other people—with *men*—could bring those same feelings of pleasure.

And that kiss had certainly been...

Well, pleasurable and the heat between them increasing in magnitude until she'd felt like she'd extended a hand too close to the stove.

And gotten burned.

Or maybe...was going to *get* burned.

Either way, now they were cleaning and then they'd each go home. Or maybe she should offer to take him to The Dairy as a thanks for vacuuming the popcorn crumbs out of the carpet—

"Mads."

His voice made her jerk, the soda that had been in the red plastic cup sloshing over the edge, dripping down the back of her hand. "Shit," she muttered.

"Sorry, Peaches," he said, taking it from her and bringing it to the industrial-sized sink that took up one corner of the classroom-like space. The water turned on and then off and then he was back with a damp paper towel that he used to clean off her hand.

Gentle swipes.

Extracting a dry towel from his pocket and carefully rubbing away the moisture.

"Do you want to get ice cream at The Dairy?" she blurted.

Loudly.

Approximately six inches from his ear, considering he was bent over and still working away on her hand, the paper towel having disappeared and his fingers now gently massaging her hand.

His head whipped up, eyes coming to hers. And God, they were such a pretty shade of blue, the dark blue of the Bay, hints of golden sunshine reflecting off the white caps. Right then they were shimmering with emotion. "I thought you didn't like desserts." A hint of a smile. "Except for Peach Persuasion."

He knew that?

Her heart began to pound faster. "I don't." A beat. "Except for Peach Persuasion."

A finger tracing the curve of her cheek. "Then I'm thinking The Dairy isn't the place we should hit, Peaches."

"They have smoothies," she told him softly.

Huge, delicious smoothies made with fresh fruit and frozen yogurt.

That finger brushed over her skin again. "That's what you want?"

She nodded.

His expression softened. "Then yeah, Mads. I could go for ice cream."

———

Lucas put the vacuum away while she gave the room a once-over, and now she was heading toward the front door for the second time that evening.

Heading toward it as someone knocked heavily on the glass.

"Wait," Lucas said, fingers brushing lightly at her back as he slipped by her, moved ahead of her toward the door. He cupped his hands around his eyes, peered through the tinted glass. A moment later, he'd straightened, reached for the lock, flicking it open with a decisive *click*.

"Who—"

But Lucas had already opened the door...

Vivi stood in the shadows, Pascal at her back, and hell if he wasn't right about being able to find her and do it quickly. The man was a freaking miracle worker and—

The thoughts cut off because then Mads processed what she was seeing and rushed forward. "Vivi, honey," she whispered. "Shit, I—"

The girl's face was covered in bruises and cuts, one eye swollen, the corner of her mouth oozing blood.

She whipped her glare toward Pascal. "She needs a hospital."

He held up a paper bag with a local clinic's logo print on the front. "We've been to the hospital. She's fine. Antibiotics and pain medicine are inside but"—his eyes flashed—"she needs a safe place to stay."

"She's going to stay with me," Mads declared.

The tiniest glimmer of amusement in Pascal's eyes. "Kind of figured that," he said softly.

"Mads," Vivi whispered, eyes glimmering with tears.

She wrapped the girl in her arms, hating the small sound of pain her embrace caused. "Shoot, honey," she said, immediately loosening her grip. "I'm sorry. You need to be resting."

Her eyes flicked up to Pascal's and he mouthed, "Ribs."

"Who?" she mouthed back, still holding Vivi, just doing it significantly more gently and carefully.

Pascal shook his head, mouthed, "Wouldn't say."

Rage in her belly.

Because even though she hadn't admitted it, based on Vivi's response the other night, it was probably Nick.

His fists.

His boots.

His—

Oh God, please let it have ended there.

"Come on," she said. "You're coming back to my place."

Vivi shook her head. "I—"

"No arguments." She started forward, thankful when Pascal held the door for them, gaze swiveling around the darkened parking lot. "You need rest and some food in your belly. We'll figure out the rest of it in the morning, okay?"

"I need to go—"

"I'll drive you guys home," Lucas interjected and Mads was thankful for the interruption. Thankful because it stopped Vivi from arguing, gave her a few moments to make sure the alarm was armed and the door locked behind her.

Then they were walking to Lucas's car, and it did something to her insides to see it parked right next to hers.

Something she wasn't going to allow to settle too deeply.

Because Vivi needed her.

Lucas opened the back door and held it as she and Vivi crawled in.

As Pascal bent and studied the two of them, eyes unfathomable. "I'll talk to you tomorrow," he said softly.

Her hands were working to gently draw the belt over Vivi's body. "Thanks." A beat. "For everything."

He nodded.

"But," she muttered, "if you ever take her to the hospital without me again, I swear I'll gut you."

His mouth tipped up, but he didn't reply, just nodded again, shut the door, and disappeared into the shadows.

"Good?" Lucas asked quietly from the front seat.

"Yeah," she whispered and took Vivi's hand, which was trembling. "Or we will be."

The last she said to Vivi, whose stare touched briefly on Mads's before sliding away, disappearing out the window, out to the dark of night.

Mads's stomach clenched, but she just held on to Vivi's hand.

Held it through the short car ride and up the stairs to her apartment. Held it as they walked down the hall to her bedroom, and as Vivi lay in Mads's bed, trying to sleep.

Trying and failing for long, long hours.

Until exhaustion finally claimed the teenager, dragging her headlong into oblivion.

Sending a prayer to the heavens that the oblivion would be peaceful and long enough to allow Vivi to get the rest she needed, Mads slowly withdrew her hand and slipped out of the bedroom.

Lucas was in the living room, as she'd somehow known he would be.

She knew he wouldn't dip out now.

Not when there was a chance that she would need him.

Twenty-Two

LUCAS

He took one look at her face and knew that she was on the edge.

"Hey," he said quickly, setting his phone on the table and pushing up from the couch, crossing to her and pulling her into a hug before he remembered that he might need to proceed with caution.

Luckily, though, she was expecting it, or getting used to him touching her...

Or she just really needed a hug.

Her arms wrapped around his middle and held on tight, and it was just as good as he'd imagined it could be.

Better.

Because it was her hold and her scent and her breath on his skin and her warm body against his. It was her hair catching on the stubble of his beard and her nails biting lightly into his flesh. It was the way she'd been trembling, but settled the longer he held her.

She sighed, pulled back, and though he hated to let her go, he did it anyway, stepping back.

"You good, Peaches?"

Dumb question, but it seemed to snap her into motion. She pushed her hair from her face, sighed again. "No," she whispered. "But also, yeah. I'm good. She's okay, and she's here, and I'll make sure she's taken care of."

"I know you will."

She nibbled at her bottom lip. "I'm sorry about ice cream."

He touched her cheek. "It'll hold. Vivi is more important."

"Yeah, she is." But those teeth stayed pressed into a plump, pink mouth.

"It wasn't a Cheat Day"—referring to the fairly strict diet plan all of the players on the Gold followed during the season, chock-full healthy, plant-based food with only an occasional day to splurge—"so I'd just be watching you eat anyway."

Her face gentled, but only for a moment.

Because then she yawned, a deep, almost bone-breaking yawn that had him jumping into motion instead of inanely staring at her, trying to commit every moment to memory.

"You hungry?"

A shake of her head. "No."

"Come on then," he said, taking her hand, drawing her toward the couch. Today—considering time had ticked well beyond midnight in the hours since he'd arrived at the youth center, helped clean that disaster of a classroom, and hung out in the living room of the apartment while Mads took care of Vivi—was a travel day, and he needed to get his ass home, sleep for a couple of hours, and pack before meeting the bus just after dawn. But all of that could wait until he got her settled, maybe even got her to fall asleep.

"I should call the social worker," she whispered when he nudged her down onto the couch.

"It's the middle of the night, baby. That can wait until morning."

She blinked, head cocking as she seemed to process that. Then she nodded. "Yeah," she whispered. "You're right."

"I know I am," he teased lightly. He nudged her back onto the cushions, swept up her feet and settled them onto the seat so she was fully reclined. Shoes off, blanket that had been folded and laid out on the sofa's arm shaken out and spread over her body, a pillow tucked behind her head.

Lids drooping, she exhaled, sleep seeming to creep in and—

She sat upright, nearly knocking their heads together, her eyes flying open. "I don't have any groceries. Shit!" She reached for the blanket, started to toss it back. "I can't have a teenage girl in my house and not have any food. I was going to go tonight after work, and—"

"You guys can go in the morning."

"But she needs food before school." Her expression went frantic. "She can't learn on an empty stomach."

He had the feeling that Vivi wasn't going back to school for a while, not with those ribs and those bruises. Not to mention the fact that she'd been hiding for the last couple of weeks. "Peaches."

"She can't, Lucas," she whispered. "She has it too tough already. She needs breakfast and snacks and—" Her voice broke.

"I'll go." He gripped her shoulder, nudged her back down.

He could sleep on the plane.

Groceries. Come back and unload them. Home to pack, shower, and change then meet the bus to the airport at the practice rink.

He glanced at his watch. He could swing that timeline.

"But—"

"Peaches," he said again, this time taking her hand. "Vivi is going to need you coherent tomorrow. That means you need sleep. I'll take care of food."

"But what if you don't get anything she likes?"

"I'll stock up on junk food." He chuckled. "You know the guys like to tease me about my favorite food being dino nuggets and tater tots."

Because they were fucking delicious.

Unfortunately, the worry didn't leave her face.

"And veggies and fruit and lean protein too."

She sighed in relief.

"Now"—he tucked her back beneath the blanket—"tell me where your spare key is."

She blinked then asked softly, "You're really going to go to the grocery store in the middle of the night to buy junk food for a teenager you don't know?"

He touched her cheek. "And fruit, veggies, and lean protein," he said lightly. "Now, Peaches. Your spare key."

He knew the locksmith had given her one.

He'd paid through the nose for it.

"Hanging on the hooks in the kitchen. It's got a blue Lego guy key chain."

His lips twitched. "Sammy?" he asked.

"Sam," she corrected gently. "But yeah."

"Kid's growing up too fast."

"Yeah," she agreed. "He is." And then she smiled and it was so beautiful, it took his breath away for a moment. "Lucas?" she asked, and he blinked, realized he'd been staring at her like a goof for however many minutes.

"Yeah?" He pushed up to his feet, turned for the kitchen.

"Thanks."

He turned back, bent and touched her cheek. "Anything," he murmured. "Anytime, yeah?"

She swallowed, eyes glimmering then nodded. "Yeah," she whispered.

Allowing himself one more moment of contact before straightening, heading for the rack of keys in the kitchen, and finding the blue minifigure with ease. He started for the door.

"Lucas?"

His mouth quirked and he spun to face her. "Yeah, baby?"

A pause. Then, "There are reusable bags under the sink."

Of course there were. Grinning now, he moved to the sink, opened the cabinet, something warming in his chest when he saw they were tucked neatly into a bag organizer. Meanwhile, *he* had an entire cupboard's worth of bags shoved into and on top of each other because he never remembered his totes and always had to buy new ones (or make the shopping cart push of shame to stash his naked groceries in his trunk and make the drive home with them rolling over each other and the entire back of his SUV). No matter that they'd been required in stores for years now, or at least for as long as he'd lived in San Francisco.

He tugged out a couple of bags, made a mental note to make sure they made it off his front seat and into the store with him.

Then started for the door again, making it as far as placing his hand on the handle this time.

"Lucas?"

Laughing now, he turned back. "Yeah?"

But his amusement faded when he took in her face.

"What is it, Peaches?"

"Will you..." A sigh. "Will you tell Ben tomorrow"—a shake of her head—"or later today? I don't want to wake him up, what with the ba—" She pressed her lips flat, released them.

"He told the team about the baby, Peaches," he said softly. "Kind of hard to keep it secret with Sammy and Marcus knowing and that baby bump of hers."

"Right. Of course. Uh. Good. I—" A breath. "Anyway, I, uh, I think he'll be relieved to know..." Her eyes flicked down the hall. "Vivi is okay."

"He will."

Silence fell between them, and slowly he reached for the knob again, pausing when his fingers connected with the metal and glancing back. "Nothing else?"

Her expression lightened. "Nothing else."

"Sleep, Mads. I'll be back soon."

Twenty-Three

MADS

Crinkles woke her.

Peeling back her lids, she winced against the bright sunlight pouring in through the windows.

Moving slowly—because, holy balls, but her couch was not comfortable for sleeping—she sat up.

Watching a couple of episodes of trash TV?

Absolutely.

But hours of vertical rest?

Nope.

And was this getting old?

Losing her ability to sleep anywhere?

Wasn't she a pampered princess?

Crinkle. Crinkle.

Smothering a sigh, she turned and spied Vivi in the kitchen. She hadn't expected to be able to fall asleep, not with knowing that Lucas was going to come back and need help with the groceries. Certainly not with Vivi bruised and battered down the hall.

But clearly, she *had* fallen asleep.

"Hey," she said, once she'd staggered to her feet and made her way into the kitchen.

Vivi glanced up from the bowl of cereal that looked more like dessert than nutritious breakfast. The colorful pieces were coated with a hazy glaze of sugar substance and the marshmallows were fluorescent.

The entire thing made Mads's teeth hurt.

But Vivi was going to town on it.

So clearly Lucas knew how to buy the proper type of junk food for teenagers who'd been through hell and back.

"Hey," Vivi said back, spooning up cereal like her life depended on it.

"I see you found the food," she teased when Vivi went to pour a second bowl.

Vivi's expression edged into panic. "I—" Her gaze darted around. "The note your hockey player left in the bathroom said to help myself. I"—she started closing up the box—"I'll stop right now. I didn't eat that much. I swear."

"Viv," Mads said gently, staying the girl's hands. "I'm sorry. I was joking. The food's for you"—a ghost of a smile—"the sugary junk food, anyway. I don't like sweets, remember?" She opened the box back up, poured Vivi another bowl. "Lucas got them for you."

Lucas who had bought food and left a note in the bathroom —but not in the bedroom because that would be creepy, a grown man entering a bedroom with a vulnerable, sleeping teenage girl he didn't know. Lucas who'd bought crappy, sugar-filled cereal that clearly hit the spot, considering how quickly it disappeared into Vivi's stomach.

When Vivi began eating again, she explained, "He made a grocery run before he left last night. Which is why I can present to you"—she swept an arm out—"*duh-duh-duh!* Cabinets with actual food in them."

Vivi smiled, just a little bit.

But that smile made Mads feel like jumping up in the air, fist pumping, *whoop* on her tongue.

Instead, though, she tried to play it cool.

"I'll just let you finish that," she said, moving to the fridge. "While I eat something that isn't neon green."

Vivi giggled, shook her head. "You don't know what you're missing."

"Preservatives," she quipped.

And earned another smile that filled her veins with champagne bubbles of joy and relief and...gratitude.

That Vivi was okay.

"After breakfast, I'll dig out some clothes for you and you can shower."

Vivi barely missed a beat in shoveling cereal into her mouth. "Lucas bought me some." She nodded down the hall. "They're in the bathroom."

Lucas being thoughtful.

Again.

Anything. Anytime.

Lucas showing her what he did with the second chance.

Again.

Anything. Anytime.

Lucas being...*Lucas.*

Her eyes stung, but she kept her tone neutral—or hoped she did anyway. "Preservatives you can keep. The other stuff we'll have to share. Including"—her heart pulsed again as she pulled out a piece of fruit—"the peaches."

Peaches.

Peaches.

She smiled...and apparently seriously failed at that whole neutral tone thing because Vivi put her fork down and studied Mads closely.

"You like him, huh?"

Mads's cheeks grew hot as she shook her head. "He's just a friend."

Who she kissed and who made her tummy feel all fluttery inside.

"Hmm."

"What?" Mads asked.

Vivi just shook her head, kept shoveling her cereal into her mouth. "Nothing," she said around a huge bite.

"I—" Mads clamped her lips together, letting that lie, knowing that she and Vivi had enough on their plates to deal with and she didn't need to add her complicated feelings about Lucas to the mix.

Only...she held a peach in her palm that he'd bought for her.

Without her asking.

More feelings.

More flutters in her tummy.

More complications.

She still took the peach to the sink and washed it...then ate every bite of succulent, juicy flesh.

The sweet residue it left on her tongue was the best thing she'd ever tasted.

And then she found herself wrapping the pit in a damp paper towel, sealing it in a ziptop bag, and placing it in the fridge.

Wondering.

If she planted that seed, could something real and strong and beautiful grow?

———

"I'm sorry to say that it's not possible for Olivia to stay here," the social worker, Donna, said, thankfully waiting until she and Mads had stepped out into the hall.

"I know it's not a permanent solution," Mads said quickly. "But you saw her. It's not safe for her to go home."

"No, it's not." Donna flipped through the papers on her clipboard, sighed. "There are a couple of other next of kins listed here.

I'll start with them, but if none will take her, then she'll have to go to a group home."

One of the few horrors that Mads hadn't experienced.

One she didn't want for Vivi.

She closed her eyes, rubbed at her temples, at the throbbing that was beginning to develop there.

"You know I like you, Mads."

Mads *hadn't* known that, actually. She'd worked a little with Donna at the center, but the other woman was a hard ass.

That was something Mads respected.

Donna went to bat for her kids, same as Mads.

How could she *not* respect that?

"I like you too, Donna," she said into the silence that fell after that declaration.

Donna's mouth quirked. "And I know Vivi is comfortable with you." A beat. "And attached to you."

"Yeah," Mads agreed.

"But even putting aside the fact that your apartment is only one bedroom"—a no-no since one of the requirements was that Vivi needed her own space—"you've got a record."

Mads sucked in a breath, eyes sliding closed. "It's only one misdemeanor."

Donna shook her head, expression contrite. "I know you've come a long way and Margie would vouch for you, but the fact is that you don't look like a solid candidate for Olivia, especially because you don't have a blood relationship." She flipped back the papers on her clipboard. "Maybe if you were married, I might be able to sweet-talk the judge and make something happen." A sigh. "But you're not married. You're single. And you have a record. And your apartment is unsuitable."

Mads's gut had been sinking this entire conversation, but that last recital really stabbed her in the heart.

Donna might as well have said *she* was unsuitable.

As a person.

Donna tucked her clipboard beneath her arm, squeezed

Mads's shoulder. "How about this? I'll get on the next of kin, okay? We'll find somewhere safe for her and in the meantime, she's here with you." She dropped her hand back to her side. "Does that work for you?"

Mads didn't really have another choice, did she?

But she needed all the goodwill she could foster with Donna, needed the social worker's help with more than just Vivi, so she just forced a smile, nodded, and thanked the other woman, waving goodbye before slipping back into her apartment.

Where Vivi was sitting on the couch, streaming YouTube and pounding junk food like her life depended on it.

She moved into the kitchen, opened her laptop, and waited to hear back from Donna.

And the phone call, hours later, made Mads's stomach sink.

Because she'd promised herself that she would protect Vivi.

And she wasn't so sure that she could keep that promise when she broke the news and Vivi took the blow that she would have to leave as she always took the shitty situations launched her way—unwaveringly and with minimal emotion.

Though she did ask if she could take the box of cereal with her.

Mads packed it and the rest of the junk food, the clothes that Lucas had bought, and then she dropped Vivi at her aunt's.

Who seemed nice enough and said all the right things when Mads walked Vivi in.

But it didn't feel right, leaving Vivi there.

And that was why, ultimately, she was worried she would fail Vivi in the end.

Had *already* failed her.

Twenty-Four

Lucas

H e was on the ice, but his focus was in the stands.

Because Mads was there.

And she looked pale, drawn out, and awful.

The preseason game had gone fine. Brit was in expert form, he'd played a few shifts, but it was mostly about getting the new players rolled into the system, helping the lines gel, giving the coaches another chance to figure out where to slot in anyone they might be moving into a permanent roster position.

Now it was two days later and they were back in San Francisco. His ass was on the bench, playing the final preseason game of the season—at least for him. The team still had a couple in the next week before the actual season got under way, but they would be rotated through the remainder of the roster.

Everyone getting some time.

The rookies and new guys getting extra.

But because this game was less for him and more for the new guys, Lucas was sitting on the bench more than normal.

Which meant he had more time to stare out into the stands.

Toward the seat that was Mads's.

She was a season ticket holder—something he'd thought that Ben had paid for. Something he'd been wrong about—because of course he had.

Still, she was seated about ten rows back from center ice, right in his line of sight.

And it looked like she hadn't slept in the last two days.

Even though she'd promised him that she had and that she was fine when they'd texted—

"You keep staring at my sister and we're going to have a problem," Ben rumbled in his ear.

Lucas jerked his gaze away, slanted a look at his teammate, opened his mouth to say...something.

"Save it," Ben muttered. "I know all about the bullshit we spin when it comes to justifying dating a teammate's sister."

Rome, on his other side, snorted. "Which means you already know you have a problem."

Lucas wished that Rome was within arm's reach.

Because he would have socked the fucker.

The tendons of Ben's bare hand stood out in sharp relief as he drank from the water bottle.

"I don't like it," Ben told him as players jumped onto the ice and others hopped off, the rest of the guys on the bench shifting down toward the door that was closer to the offensive zone. "I sure as *shit* don't like it"—a glare Lucas's way—"but I get it." His eyes narrowed further. "Still, if you hurt her..."

The threat didn't need to be finished.

"I won't."

He had. He wouldn't. Not ever again.

His eyes went back to her in the stands, to that pale skin and those dark circles visible even from across the rink.

"But who did?" he muttered.

Ben chucked the water bottle back into the holder. "The social worker wouldn't let Vivi stay at Mads's place."

"What?" She hadn't told him that. "Why not?"

"She—"

The guys they were changing for started peeling off the play, hauling ass toward the bench. Ben stood up, leaped over the boards, and Lucas followed suit, immediately in the rush of the game, immediately jumping into the action. All his focus went to hockey, to the puck and open lanes, toward trying to get a good chance on goal.

Avoiding collisions and finishing checks.

Connecting passes.

They made it back to the bench, but Coach Calle switched up the lines, pairing him with two young rookies and making it so he didn't get a chance to finish his conversation with Ben. And when the game finished, Ben was pulled aside for media.

"Fuck it," Lucas muttered, shoving his sticks onto the rack and rushing through the process of getting undressed.

Mads always hung around after games—something he'd thought was manipulative and annoying before, something that he was grateful for that night.

He'd go to her, get some answers.

Figure out what was wrong.

And then he'd sort out how to fix it.

————

Fans didn't often see players running through the parking lot, searching for a shitty ass car that Ben had complained about Mads not letting him replace more than once.

Something else Lucas had thought was manipulation.

Something *else* Lucas now just got was Mads.

Wanting to make her own way.

But she wasn't in this situation with Vivi alone, and he was going to make damned sure she knew that, even if he was stopped quite a few times in his search of the old rust bucket, cursing that this was the one time she'd decided to leave without seeing Ben. Something that spoke of how upset she was.

Something that had his gut churning and him moving faster.

Luckily, he had a general idea of where she parked, but general wasn't exact, especially when he was dealing with twenty thousand fans pouring out of the stadium and dispersing onto public transit, Lyfts, and their own cars.

Eventually, though, he spotted her climbing into the driver's seat of her car and picked up his pace. "Mads!" he called.

She froze, glanced back at him, those shadows under her eyes even darker under the dim lights of the parking lot. Her body was tense, clearly ready to escape, but then she seemed to process that it was him shouting at her. "Lucas," she said softly as he closed in on her. "What are you doing here?"

"What's wrong?"

Her head jerked back. "I'm fine."

He cupped her cheek, moving without thinking, thankful that she didn't flinch, that she actually leaned into his touch, his hold. "Peaches, what the fuck happened with Vivi?"

She jerked again, but this time it was to pull out of his hold. She looked away, and he watched her throat work, saw the glimmer of tears in her eyes. "She's fine," she whispered. "Or at least she's pretending to be. She's with her aunt."

"But why isn't she with you?"

Vivi was clearly attached to Mads. He'd seen that in the way she'd clung to Mads that night, the way she'd all but crawled into her lap on the drive back to the apartment. He'd seen it before too, when he'd volunteered, when he'd seen the way the girl had lingered near Mads during events, like she and Mads were kindred spirits.

He hated that it was probably true.

Mads sighed, shifting to close the driver's side door and leaning back against it. "The social worker said that I'm not an acceptable temporary foster parent."

Her voice was quiet. Small.

Her demeanor was the same...along with a dash of defeated.

"Why?"

A shake of her head. "It doesn't matter."

"Why, Peaches?" he pressed.

A sigh. "My apartment is only one bedroom and I have a misdemeanor on my record."

His brows came up.

"The first is obvious. The second—" She cleared her throat. "Well, I got in trouble right after I left home," she said hurriedly. "I was broke and hungry and you already know that I stole. This time I did it stupidly." She pressed her lips together, released them. "I was so damned hungry, but that's no excuse. I knew better, even back then."

"Peaches."

"And I had a public defender, and he told me to plead guilty. I wouldn't get any jail time, and I could move on. It made sense at the time." She sighed. "But seriously, for all the illegal stuff I did in my life—and I did far more than my fair share—I got caught stealing a couple of candy bars. Stupid, huh?" she whispered. "And now it's part of the reason that I can't help Vivi," she said, hands clenching into fists, voice growing louder. "She doesn't like her aunt. I could tell when I dropped her off, and if things go bad there and she can't go home safely, then she's back out on the streets and *I don't want that for her.*" Her head hung. "But I'm afraid that she's going to end up there anyway."

Yeah, no.

That wasn't happening.

"I can talk to the team's attorney," he told her. "See if we can get your record expunged."

Her eyes went wide.

"She's awesome, and she has connections. I bet we can explain, and she'd find a way to have that off your record in no time."

"I—"

"And as far as your apartment goes, I know Ben knows the leasing manager"—that was why he'd chosen the complex for his sister in the first place—"I bet they can work out a transfer to a two-bedroom, especially given the circumstances."

"Lucas, I—"

"That will solve the record and the apartment and you can take Vivi—"

"No, I can't," she whispered.

"Mads."

She shook her head. "I can't."

"Peaches," he told her. "We'll make it work—"

"I'm not married."

He rocked back on his heels, heart starting to pound. "What?"

"I'm not married. I'm single. Donna said I'm not married and with everything else, I'm—" A shake of her head, gaze drifting down to her feet. "I'm just...not married."

"Okay," he said, heart pounding even faster now, pieces lining up in his mind.

He could help her.

He could do this.

He—

"Let's get married."

TWENTY-FIVE

MADS

"This is insane," she whispered as she stared at herself in the mirror, eyes wide and bordering on panicked.

But she still picked up the tube of lipstick and spread it over her mouth, painting her lips a deep burgundy.

That went with the rest of her makeup.

And the long curls she'd spent hours fussing with until they cascaded down her back in sleek, shining twists of hair. And...

With the white dress she'd picked up at a shop down the street.

Probably the single most beautiful piece of clothing she'd ever owned. More ivory than brilliant white and falling just above her knee, it clung to her curves, accentuating her bust, skimming over her torso, flaring out from her hips. And that didn't even mention the sparkle. Dashes of it along the sweetheart neckline, skating down her stomach, sprinkled throughout the tulle that swung around her legs as she walked.

It was Vegas Princess.

And she loved it.

And—

"This is insane."

But she capped the lipstick, stashed it in the purse she'd fought with Lucas about.

Because he'd seen her looking at it and had the attendant grab it off the shelf. Just like he'd seen her looking at the dress through the window and had drawn her into the store, despite her protests that she didn't need a dress for a fake wedding. The purse—and the heels that were sitting in a box on the edge of the bed, even though she'd been very careful to avoid looking at them for too long—had become hers.

She didn't need any of this.

She needed a husband. She needed all of the roadblocks that Donna said were in the way gone.

And she needed Vivi safe.

Not a fancy dress that had nearly made her pass out from the cost and heels and a purse that were each as insanely overpriced.

Not a chartered plane to Vegas in the hours after Lucas had blurted out a proposal in the parking lot of the arena.

Not a hotel room that had multiple bedrooms and overlooked the famous fountains on the strip.

Not room service to fill her belly as he'd left to give her time to get ready and so he could talk to the lawyer the Gold's attorney had recommended.

To expunge her record.

"This is insane," she whispered again. But it was an insane kind of fairy tale, flying here, doing this, wearing this dress.

Letting Lucas help her.

By getting married.

By. Getting. Married.

Oh, fuck. What was she doing?

She pushed up from the upholstered seat she'd been kneeling on as she leaned closer to carefully apply her lipstick, panic beginning to eat away at her insides. Lipstick. A dress. Heels and a purse. A marriage that was in name only so she could be a foster mom for a teen she barely knew—

Yeah, no. She couldn't do this. It was *literally* insane.

She needed to go. She needed—

Click.

She heard the door to the hotel room open, footsteps on the tile-lined hall floor. Footsteps that became muffled as, presumably, Lucas hit the carpet outside the bedroom she was getting ready in.

"Peaches?"

Shit. *Shit.*

She glanced around the room, looking for an escape route. But there wasn't one. Even the wide window next to the bed didn't open.

The only way out was the door—

That Lucas was striding through.

Her belly fluttered, heart rolling over in her chest.

God, he was beautiful. His thickly muscled body clad in a gray suit that had to have been custom-made for him. Something he must have picked up from his house when they'd stopped there on the way to the airport.

Snug around his shoulders, sinfully tight around his thighs, it contrasted beautifully with the crisp white shirt that was unbuttoned at the collar.

Giving her a glimpse of a tan throat, the faintest sprinkling of dark hair.

That throat worked, and she realized he'd stopped dead.

And suddenly she was nervous.

"Fuck, Mads," he rasped. "You're beautiful."

It was like her lungs inflated in an instant, so fast that oxygen swept toward her brain in a rush that made her feel dizzy.

Or maybe it was the way he was looking at her.

Like she *was* the most beautiful woman he'd ever seen.

He held two ties in one hand and a bouquet of flowers in his other.

The ties he tossed on the back of the chair. The flowers he gently handed to her before lightly stroking the backs of his knuckles over her cheek. "Hope these are okay."

Okay.

Okay?

She didn't know if she should melt into a blubbering puddle on the ground or lean into the whole escape route...well, *route*, and run screaming from the room. "I—"

His phone rang and he tugged it out. "Sorry," he told her before glancing at the screen. "I think it's the attorney legal recommended." A swipe. "Hello? Yes, this is Lucas Clark. Bec Darden, right? Thanks so much for the call back."

Mads's eyes went wide.

Bec Darden. *The* Bec Darden.

She was one of the most famous lawyers in San Francisco.

"Yeah. It's just the one, and she works at the..." He named the youth center and Mads tuned back in, mind scrambling to process and keep up at the same time. "Uh-huh, she's trying to find a way to foster one of the kids there. Right." He paced away. "Yeah, we're working on both of those things right now." Then he rotated around, his eyes shooting to hers and turning that fluttering in her belly into a tornado. "Really?" he asked softly. "You can get it cleared off that easily?"

Mads sucked in a breath.

"By Monday?"

Held the air in her lungs for so long she would have forgotten to breathe if Lucas hadn't come over and taken her hand, hadn't squeezed it lightly. Only then did the breath hiss out of her as she wavered on the pretty, sparkly heels he'd bought her.

Lucas wrapped an arm around her, tucked her close. "You're a miracle worker. I don't how to thank you..."

A moment of quiet as he listened.

Then the soft chuckle vibrated through his body and into hers. "I will definitely be making a sizable donation to that charity."

Haze clearing, Mads stiffened, slipped out from beneath his arm as he continued talking, worry gnawing at her insides.

Worry that didn't ease when she spotted the bouquet—a

gorgeous grouping of roses that were such a pale shade of pink they were almost white. And there were tiny sparkling crystals tucked between each of the flowers, a glittering ribbon wrapped around the stems.

Beautiful.

Perfect.

Not for her.

"Peaches."

He was close and behind her and she hadn't heard him end the call. Hadn't felt him come up.

But by some miracle she didn't freak out, didn't shut down.

As though maybe her body knew his.

Or maybe...her heart knew his—

"I don't need any of this," she blurted.

"What?"

"The dress. The shoes. The purse." She swept out a hand. "The *flowers*. I don't need any of it."

"You deserve it, though."

"But it's not real. None of it's real"—she set the bouquet on the table, gently because it was fucking beautiful and she didn't want to ruin it, not like she'd ruined so many other things—"and I don't need it and—"

She clenched her hands into fists, tried to calm down.

But the worry in her belly had clawed up her throat.

Lucas stepped close, his expression conflicted, and it seemed like he wanted to argue with her. But after a moment, his face cleared and he gently touched her cheek. "The pictures need to look real, right? Just in case the social worker and judge need proof."

Oh. Right.

That made sense.

And it was also...oddly disappointing.

"Which means you need a dress and flowers and we need to look like this wasn't rushed. Like we're stable."

But it *was* rushed.

And it had the likelihood of crumpling like a deck of cards trying to withstand a tornado.

"And Vivi needs you."

That quelled the panic.

"Yeah," she finally murmured. "Vivi needs me."

He slipped a finger beneath her chin, tilted her head up, holding her gaze like he could see into the very depths of her soul. "We'll be okay."

She exhaled, much of her anxiety leaving on that puff of air. "Yeah. We'll be okay."

Her. Vivi.

Lucas.

God, she hoped so. Because if not—

He dropped his hand, picked up the ties. "Now, tell me. Pink or gray?"

Her gaze flicked between the strips of silk and the open fabric at the base of his throat. The smooth skin she wanted to touch.

To stroke.

To kiss.

Fake. It was all fake—even if some long-buried part of her heart pulsed at the thought.

But it was for Vivi, so she smiled, shored herself up, took the ties from him, and tossed them over the back of the chair.

"Neither."

And then she walked from the room.

It was time to get married.

Twenty-Six

LUCAS

"I now pronounce you husband and wife," Elvis told them. "You may kiss the bride."

His first thought was that Ben was seriously going to murder him.

His second was that he hadn't thought it possible for Mads to look more beautiful. But standing next to him, her wide eyes on his, her makeup and hair gorgeous, that dress...something out of a fucking fantasy, and he knew that he would never forget a second of it.

Each detail was committed to memory.

The curl sliding forward to curve around her cheek.

The pink tip of her tongue dipping out, leaving her bottom lip glistening.

The way the net-like material on the lower half of her dress caught at the fabric of his pants.

The scent of flowers coating the air, and not from the bouquet she clung to. It was just Mads, soft and sweet and *his*.

With a glimmering diamond on her finger.

Something she would have certainly argued with him about if

not for Elvis standing in front of them as the King of Rock and Roll had instructed them on reciting the vows.

She didn't *need* it.

But he needed her to have it.

Even if this was happening because she needed a husband and not because she needed *him*.

Her hands tightened on the bouquet, and he realized he'd been so focused on absorbing every detail that he'd forgotten Elvis's order.

"Okay?" he asked softly.

She nibbled at her bottom lip but nodded.

He leaned in, pressed his mouth to hers...

And all hell broke loose.

Inside his head.

His heart.

Less so with the outside world.

Because the moment his lips touched Mads's, the rest of the universe fell away as a thousand more details began branding themselves to his mind, his senses. The sharp edges of the crystals sewn into her skirt pressing into his palms, the roughness of that netting material beneath his fingers. The plumpness of her mouth under his. The softness of her body against him. The curve of her ass as his hand sought out the lush *peach*. The taste of that succulent fruit on his tongue.

Because he'd made sure there was a basket of them in the limo they'd taken over, made sure she'd eaten one.

Her soft moan vibrating through his chest.

Her hands settling on his shoulders, fingernails kneading into his flesh.

Keeping him close when he should pull away.

Hips brushing his, pelvis lining up perfectly with his. He slid his hand down, found the edge of that netted material, the silken skin underneath, and began inching his fingers up—

A hand on his shoulder, startling him. "And thank you, thank you very much."

Said in that shitty ass accent.

Making Lucas remember exactly where he was.

And where his *hand* was.

"Shit," he muttered, pulling back, slipping his hand out from beneath her skirt, gently disengaging her hold on his shoulders. "Peaches," he murmured when she just leaned into him heavier, eyes still closed.

Slowly, those lids peeled back open and the dazed look in her deep brown eyes was another thing he would remember forever.

"Come on, baby," he said gently, winding his arm around her waist, keeping her close as she stared up at him.

A flash drew his gaze, and he saw one of the witnesses he'd paid for had a camera.

"Smile!" she called.

There was another flash.

He glanced back down, saw that the daze had started to clear from Mads's expression. But the softness didn't, and she didn't pull away from him when the woman demanded they smile again and there was another flash.

"Got it!" she called, disappearing out into the lobby, presumably to print the pictures.

"You good?" he asked, craning his neck so he could see Mads's face.

"Yeah," she whispered.

He nodded his thanks to Elvis and started leading her out of the room, committing the way she held his hand so tightly to memory along with everything else.

The pictures were in a bag by the time they made it out and then they were in the back of the limo he'd rented.

And...silence.

Mads clutching the bouquet, the bag of pictures on the seat next to her.

And...they were married.

Ben was going to kill him, and, objectively, it was an unreasonable thing to do—to get married so Mads could be a foster parent, to get married when they'd kissed *once*. To get married when he was just beginning to prove to her that he wasn't an asshole.

And when he wasn't entirely sure he'd succeeded in *proving* that.

So, yeah, it was a crazy thing to do and he wasn't sure it was the *right* thing to do. But he *was* sure that he would do anything to see the expression on her face when he'd convinced her to come to Vegas and do this for Vivi's sake. It was the same look she'd given him when he'd offered to reach out to the team's lawyers and when he'd told her about Bec Darden taking on the task of expunging her record.

The same look that came from him giving her the bouquet. The dress. The shoes.

The ring he'd slipped on her finger just minutes before.

She hadn't ever been spoiled—not growing up with a mom who didn't have her shit together and dad who'd disappeared on her and a brother who loved her but wasn't much older than her. Ben had done what he could, but Lucas knew that it had been a struggle. And that was before Ben left.

Before everything went bad.

No. *Worse.*

And she wasn't spoiled now, working long hours for minimal pay, refusing her brother's help even though he was more than willing to give it.

Well, shit was going to change.

And not just because he'd married her.

Because she deserved it.

"Lucas?" she asked, drawing his gaze from where it had drifted out the window, watching the lights of the Strip flash by, thinking that he'd fucked up because he hadn't thought past the wedding, and now he was wondering where in the fuck he was going to take her the night of her wedding when she was a recovering addict.

Not drinking or gambling or to partake in a bit of the green stuff from one of the dispensaries on the Strip.

Not back to the hotel room to fuck her brains out.

"Yeah, Peaches?" he asked, turning back to face her.

"Are you having regrets about doing this?"

"No." He took her hand. "Not even one."

"But..." She trailed off, shook her head.

"What?"

"But how?"

He didn't have any regrets.

Maybe he should.

But he didn't. Because she was his *now*. She was his *future*. And he was going to spoil the shit out of her and bust his ass to make sure she gave him that soft look each and every day.

"I regret a lot of things with you," he murmured, reaching over taking her hand. "So many fucking things when it comes to how I treated you—"

She inhaled, mouth opening.

"But this will never be one of those."

Her exhale was shuddering.

Her face went soft.

And suddenly he knew exactly where he was going to take her. He tugged out his phone, typed out a text, and called in a favor.

Then leaned forward and knocked on the glass divider.

TWENTY-SEVEN

MADS

The wind whipped her hair around as Lucas drew her forward.

It was dark beneath the blindfold—beneath the gray tie he'd never put on but had apparently stashed in his pocket. A tie that was now secured around her head, covering her eyes. Something he'd done shortly after they'd arrived in a darkened parking garage, leaving her in the car with the promise of "Be right back."

She'd heard the soft rumble of his voice through the closed door and windows and just when she was really starting to worry, he'd come back, murmuring softly, "It's me," as he opened the door, immediately putting her at ease.

Then he'd taken her hand, helped her out of the car.

Into an elevator.

Down a carpeted hall.

Through a series of doors.

And now she was outside again, the wind raising goose bumps on her skin.

Lucas squeezed her fingers. "You okay?"

"Aside from the fact that I can't see where I'm going?"

A chuckle that slid like silk down between her breasts, over her belly, between her thighs. "Yeah, Peaches, aside from that." He dropped her hand, placed his on her hips and lifted her, stealing her breath.

But just as quickly, she was on her feet again, heels clicking on the tile again.

"I'm fine," she said through her rapidly increasing pulse, through her heart beating in the back of her throat.

Startled but not scared.

More than a little turned on, absolutely.

And also a bit cold from the wind whipping around, sending her hair flying, her skirt clinging to her thighs as she was led forward, but no sooner had the thought crossed her mind than Lucas's jacket was settling around her shoulders.

Warm. Spicy. *Lucas.*

She inhaled, telling herself that the gesture shouldn't matter. He was just being nice, trying to make up for all the shit he'd given her.

It was just that she wanted...

For it to be real.

Silly, huh? Her life wasn't a fairy tale, and she wasn't a woman who'd stepped out from between the pages of a romance novel, getting her hottie of a hockey player to fall in love with her.

This was just...

Fake.

And still, she didn't want him to be with her because he felt bad, because it was a convenient marriage that would make it so she could help Vivi. She didn't want it to be pretend.

Some delusional part of her wanted it to be real.

That a man would make this effort for *her.*

If it's not for you, Mads, then who the fuck is he making the effort for?

She bit down on the edge of her tongue.

Because she couldn't explain *that* away, same as she couldn't explain why she'd made this crazy leap and flown to Vegas.

Except, it was for Vivi.

Except...it was also for her.

Before she could truly process that, Lucas took off the blindfold and the scene in front of her made every thought of *fake* fall away.

Her vision immediately went blurry as tears flooded her eyes.

Her heart couldn't take it.

"What is this?" she rasped.

He shrugged—*shrugged!*—like what she was seeing was no big deal. After the bouquet and dress and purse and heels. After the kiss in front of Elvis. After Bec Darden working on her record and calling the leasing office and...after *this*. "I have a buddy who played for Vegas for a couple of seasons. He didn't want the responsibility of a house, so he lived here."

Here being a freaking penthouse, apparently taking up an entire corner of one of the hotels that overlooked the sparkling lights of the Strip, the huge glass-encased balcony ...and filled with a low table and a cozy couch. And flowers and candles and twinkly lights strung overhead. And soft music played in the background.

Rose petals on the tiles all around them, their floral scent in her nose.

And a warm jacket around her shoulders.

"Obviously," Lucas went on, "he owed me a couple of favors."

"A *couple?*"

He tugged lightly at a strand of her hair. "Yeah, baby, just a couple." Then he took her hand, led her over to the couch that was positioned behind the low table laden with fruit and cheese and vegetables. Not a gram of processed sugar in sight.

Her heart couldn't take *this*.

"Lucas," she whispered.

"Yeah, Peaches?"

"This is—"

A finger to her lips. "It's not too much."

Throat tight, she shook her head. "I don't know how to process this, to *deal* with this. The view"—she swept out a hand at the gorgeous skyline—"the dress. This whole situation, it's…"

"Insane."

That didn't loosen the knot in her throat.

In fact, it grew in magnitude, threatened to choke her.

"But it somehow feels right," he murmured. "Doesn't it?"

It *did* feel right, and that was the part that was hardest to accept. Because it wasn't logical or smart or—

"Do you know why I hated you so much at first?"

"You're protective of Ben." She fussed with the hem of her dress. "He's not just your teammate, he's your friend, and I was messing with his life."

"Yeah," he said. "That's part of it for sure. But you know I couldn't let it go after you two had reconciled, not like the other guys did."

Because he'd grown up with people who did what she had, who he thought had done worse than her.

"You never did it in front of Ben, though."

A self-deprecating laugh. "You think he'd put up with that shit?"

She smiled. "No, he wouldn't."

"So, I was an asshole, but at least I wasn't a stupid one."

"I did bad things," she said. "It wasn't unwarranted."

"Just because I grew up in a family of addicts who never missed a chance to fuck up my life, to try and suck me dry, it doesn't mean that I should have treated you like that."

That sent a bolt of pain through her.

Fuck up my life. Try and suck me dry.

Because she'd done that to Ben. Because she knew how much that hurt her brother, how much it must have—must *still*—hurt Lucas.

But it was more important they move past this. All the dirty details (and her battle with her guilt) could happen later.

She covered his hand, squeezed lightly. "You've apologized. We've acknowledged the asshole and you've shown me that you're not going to be that man anymore—"

"You're being too fucking nice about it," he muttered, shoving his free hand through his hair. "You should be pissed at me for eternity."

"Would that make you feel better?" she asked, genuinely curious.

He paused, considered that. "Yeah, actually it would."

"And you don't think what you're doing more than makes up for how you treated me?"

"No, it doesn't." That hand shoved through his hair again. "It *doesn't*. Nothing excuses it—"

"Tell me about your family."

He froze, panic in his gorgeous blue eyes. "Mads. It's not an excuse."

"My dad left, and my mom is fucking clueless." A sigh. "You know that much." Her heart began pounding, but she pushed on. She needed him to know exactly what she'd done. Maybe then he would forgive himself and they could move on. "She lost it when Ben left, went out partying, got married without me even meeting the guy. And"—the memories clawed their way up her throat, turning her voice raspy—"when he moved in, he—"

"Peaches, you don't have to—"

She'd said the words in rehab, in therapy, to Ben, to Lily, to Margie.

She found she needed to say them to Lucas as well.

"He raped me. And my mom was too fucked up to notice that something was seriously wrong with me. Only her drug of choice wasn't oxy or booze, like me. It was fucking denial—denial that the man she'd picked was a monster, that he was hurting me, even denial that he'd raped me." A short, staccato breath. "Even though I nearly died from the abortion he made me get."

This was where she lost the stamina to keep going, feeling the hot slide of tears down her cheeks.

Feeling alone in that painful past.

But only for a second.

Because then she was in Lucas's arms and he was holding her tight, letting her sob into his chest. And probably staining that expensive suit with makeup.

He didn't tell her to hush, to not cry, to stop.

He just let her get it out.

Which was probably why the rest of it came then, a flood of words that she might have hidden if she wasn't so raw, so exposed, all of her wounds on display for Lucas to see. She was feeling so much she couldn't hold on to the fear of what he would think of her.

She just...gave him the rest.

"I ran away from home, even though my mom kicked him out. I couldn't—*can't*—stand being in the same room as her, even though I pretend it's okay for Ben's sake." Mads sighed. "And after everything happened, she did try to help me. But it was eighteen years too late to snap out of that fog, to give a shit about me." She exhaled, forced herself to go on. "After the abortion, I had complications and almost died. That's the only reason it all came out." Her hand went to her belly, a spasm of pain reminding her of what she'd lost. She'd loved that baby girl, had promised to protect her. And she hadn't. "Ben doesn't know this next part. Nobody does." She clung to the lapels of Lucas's suit but managed to straighten away from his chest, to meet his eyes. "Ben thought it was at ten weeks, but it wasn't. I-it was much l-later and done in some back alley clinic and she was a little girl and I didn't even get to hold her." Her sobs stole her voice for several long moments. "Bill"—her stepdad—"he drugged me so a lot of it is blurry, but I *remember*..."

Lucas weaved a hand into her hair, tugged her close, pressed her to his chest.

Tears poured down her face, her voice barely a whisper. "I remember the pain and the blood and asking to hold her."

"Fuck, baby, you're killing me."

"I-I'm so-sorry, I'll stop—"

Those fingers that were threaded through the strands of her hair tightened slightly, tugging her head up. "Don't you fucking dare, Peaches. These are not burdens that you need to carry alone any longer."

Mads felt those words in the very depths of her soul.

And then she was crying again, being held close again, and still Lucas didn't ask her to stop, to hush, or even order her to get it all out already.

He just...held her.

And allowed her to take what she needed from him.

"I couldn't stay in that house, so I kept running away and I started using and eventually I didn't go home at all, eventually it was easier to be high all the time because then I wouldn't feel, wouldn't remember. I ran in with Nick and his crowd, spent most of my time fucked up and—" She swallowed. "I did whatever I had to in order to get that oblivion—pills, shooting up, booze, stealing from good people like Georgia and selling their belongings to pay for that next hit. Selling *myself, my body* to do the same. Ben pulled me out more times than I can count, and even my mom did too, but I was too lost in my own misery to want to get better."

A hand stroking gently through her hair. "What changed?" he asked softly.

"I saw Ben after he was with Jordyn and I saw how happy she was making him and...I saw how miserable *I* was making him and —" A breath. "I just didn't want to keep hurting him."

"Peaches," he rasped.

"I love him, and he deserves better."

She exhaled, hating the pain in his eyes, forced herself to turn toward the positive, toward the future.

"And I'm starting to think that I deserve the same."

Twenty-Eight

LUCAS

He'd intended to tell her about his shitshow of a family.

To lay it all on the line.

Instead, she'd turned the tables on him and did that, sharing so much heavy shit it was a fucking miracle she hadn't buckled under the weight.

She'd survived.

Fuck, the thought of her crying out for a baby girl she'd obviously loved, even despite the circumstances of her conception, killed him.

His upbringing had been fucking rainbows and cotton candy in comparison.

"And I'm starting to think that I deserve the same," she whispered, her mascara smeared beneath her eyes, cheeks flushed, and lashes clinging together.

A fucking *miracle*.

"You do deserve happiness and love and respect, baby. You deserve the world."

Her eyes slid closed and she inhaled deeply, shoulders lifting then dropping on her exhale. "Lucas."

He heard it then.

The weariness. The fatigue.

The stress of the last few days catching up with her.

She was done.

So now it was time for him to take care of her. Starting with food and then rest and then getting her back to California so she could start doing what she needed to do for Vivi.

So, him sharing could wait.

He'd given her bare bones, knew she was smart enough to read between the lines, and there was more important shit than playing the Trauma Olympics.

"Time to eat, Peaches," he said, "and we're going to enjoy the lights and the cool air for as long as you want. Then we'll head back to the hotel, sleep, and catch a flight back home tomorrow."

Her eyes had peeled back open when he'd started speaking, and he watched them soften, felt her body relax against his.

"Good, baby," he murmured, stroking her hair back from her face, gently rubbing his thumb beneath both of her eyes. Her mascara appeared to be a lost cause and would require more force than he was willing to use on her delicate skin, so he just shifted her so she'd be more comfortable on the cushion next to him.

Then reached for the plate of fruit.

Still soft.

But now her lips turned up. "You really do pay attention, don't you?"

That she didn't like sweets? Yup. That she generally ate pretty healthily? Also yup. To every single detail he could glean about her to make her life easier? Absolutely.

He liked this woman, despite doing every fucking thing in his power to hate her.

He liked her. Respected her. Wanted to claim her as his own and growl at anyone else who dared to make a move on what he saw as his.

So, yeah, he was feeling more than a little feral when it came to Mads.

But it was more than caveman instincts, more than liking, more than doing her a favor by marrying her—as fucking ridiculous as that thought was.

Deep inside, he knew this woman was *his*.

Which was why all he did in that moment was offer her the plate. "Eat. Sleep. Enjoy the lights." She selected a strawberry, lifted it to her lips, mouth opening, white teeth sinking into the plump red fruit. His cock twitched, and he'd be lying if he said he didn't want those lips closing over his dick, that tongue that was currently flicking out to lap up a bead of juice on his skin. But that wasn't what she needed. "Then tomorrow," he said softly, "it's back to reality."

She chewed, studying him for long moments.

Then set the strawberry stem on the plate. "What if I'm not ready to go back to reality?" she asked softly.

He slid the plate onto the table, mouth turning up, so fucking glad to see a blip of playfulness in her eyes. Too much heavy. Too much *reality*. "We're in Vegas, baby. If there's ever a place to leave real life behind, it's the Sin City." He nodded out toward the Strip. "We can walk around, see the fountains, eat a bunch of food that's bad for us. We can go to a club and dance—"

"*You* dance?" she asked, mouth agape.

"When I have a gorgeous woman to hold close."

Her mouth curved. "Of course you do."

"What does that mean?"

"Mr. Playboy?"

He groaned, dropped his head back against the couch. "Please don't tell me you follow that TikTok account."

"Eva Moreno is amazing."

"She's a pain in my ass." He scowled. "But she's got a fucking eye for the game." A tug of Mads's hair. "Kind of like another Superwoman I know who comes to almost every Gold game."

Mads's cheeks went a little pink. "I like watching my brother play."

"And telling him what he does wrong."

Those cheeks went a little redder. "I—"

"Messing with your poor brother's game," he teased. "Getting in his head. All he talks about in the locker room is how hard he works to make you proud."

She narrowed her eyes, giving him some of the sass he'd so rarely seen from her (mostly because she'd radiated between anger and hurt and ignoring him). But he'd witnessed her dishing it out to Ben, to Lily, even occasionally, to Rome.

And now to him...which probably he shouldn't like, but *probably* didn't factor into this moment.

And...another blip in time that was committed to memory— the wind in her hair, her body close, her mouth turning up. "I guess now that we're married," she sassed, "you'd better brace because I've got *plenty* of comments on your game."

He froze.

Then busted up, cheeks hurting because his smile was so wide.

"Oh," she murmured and he sobered, glancing back at her, seeing her expression had gone serious.

"What is it, Peaches?"

"Nothing, really." She lifted a hand, touched his jaw. "I just really like making you laugh."

He inhaled sharply. "Best feeling in the world making someone you care about happy."

Her fingers stilled on his jaw. "Is that what—" She pressed her lips flat, shook her head. Then dropped her hand and reached for the plate. "We should make sure the food doesn't go to waste."

He captured her hand. "Mads."

She froze, eyes on her lap, silent for long enough that he thought she wouldn't answer. But then she did. "But that's not what this is."

His fingers spasmed.

"You're being really nice, trying to make up for something that you don't have to, being a good teammate and friend, and just generally being a really good guy, but..." She exhaled. "This isn't what that is for us. You don't care about me"—his mouth dropped open, shock radiating through him—"not like that," she added hurriedly. "I'm just the recipient of your good deeds—"

"The fuck you say?"

That wasn't exactly what he wanted to blurt out, especially when it made her teeth click together as she pulled back. "I-I—"

He captured her wrists, drew her forward, drew her back against him.

Where she belonged.

"You think I would *marry* you strictly to be a good guy?"

Her mouth opened and closed a few times. "I...um—"

"Peaches, you're hot as fuck and my dick has been broken for every other woman except you for fucking months now."

She drew in a breath.

"But that's not why I'm here, sitting next to you, a ring on my finger and a marriage certificate in the back of the limo."

An exhale. Her chin coming up. "So why *are* you here?"

TWENTY-NINE

MADS

*P*eaches, *you're hot as fuck and my dick has been broken for every other woman except you for fucking months now.*

Her heart was pounding so hard it seemed to be making its way up her throat.

"But that's not why I'm here, sitting next to you, a ring on my finger and a marriage certificate in the back of the limo."

It took everything in her to ask, "Then why? Why are you here? Why are *we* here?"

It was a question to him...and to herself.

Because...insanity.

Because insanity never felt so freaking right.

His hand squeezed hers and she stared into pools of deep blue. "You know," he murmured. She started to shake her head, but then he lifted their hands, placed them over his heart. "You feel it here, same as me."

Her throat tightened further, and she found she couldn't answer.

Could just leave her hand where it was, feel his pulse pounding against her palm, racing just like hers was.

"Not a favor," he said softly, then drew her hand down the hard muscles of his torso, not stopping until her fingers grazed the hard tip of his erection. "Not because I'm a good guy. I think I showed you that I'm far from that already—"

"No," she whispered.

He paused, brows drawn together, releasing her hands.

"If I don't get to wallow in the guilt of the bad things I've done, you don't get to either." Those brows pulled down further, mouth opening, but she went on, *pressed* on. "*No.* You don't get to keep beating yourself up." Because she had to make sure he understood, had to have them both take this step forward and move on. Otherwise, it would always feel like this to him, to her—that they were both spending their entire lives trying to make up for stuff and not actually living.

And, with the bright lights of Vegas around them, a pretty dress on her body, heels on her feet, a diamond on her finger...she thought that maybe she finally could.

If Lucas stayed here with her.

In the present.

"Peaches—"

She spun to face him. "We don't get to do that anymore."

Yes. *Exactly.* The puzzle pieces began sliding into place. Because yes, this was right and that truth settled over her like her cozy bathrobe. Warm, soft, *right.*

"No more guilt." She stood up. "No more punishing ourselves over and over and *fucking over* again."

"Mads—"

Bending, probably flashing him in the process since her dress didn't allow for a bra, realizing that considering he'd just told her his dick had only worked for her over the last months, *considering* what she'd just felt with her own fingers, he wouldn't mind a glimpse of her boobs.

And yeah, when she flicked her gaze to his, saw the heat in his eyes after he'd slowly pulled his off her chest and up to hers, he didn't mind at all.

A blossoming of heat in her belly, so strong that it almost took her by surprise.

She was no virgin.

But she'd never felt like *this*.

It was like the kiss at the altar, the first kiss they'd shared not long before that—the need she felt for this man sent her pulse skyrocketing and her stomach fluttering.

But *more*.

Heat flooding through her belly, desire soaking between her thighs.

Living.

She was *finally* living.

Which was why she held that emotion close, bent a little further, giving him more than a glimpse, and took his hand.

"Come on," she said, drawing him to his feet. "Let's go."

He lifted his brows. "Where are we going?"

She grinned.

"Dancing, Mr. Playboy."

———

The music blared all around them, lights flashing.

People were everywhere, on the dance floor, at the bar, at the high-tops dotted throughout the club. There was alcohol flowing, but she didn't smell it, didn't almost taste it on her tongue, not like she sometimes did at a party with the team, with her brother and his friends, didn't have the deep, clawing craving in her stomach.

She barely noticed it.

Because she wasn't seeking out oblivion.

She was committing everything to memory.

And lost in her latest addiction of being plastered against Lucas's body, swaying to the music, pretending that it was some-what close to the rhythm blasting out through the speakers but knowing she wasn't hearing anything except the beat of his heart beneath her ear.

Her feet were killing her.

Exhaustion was pulling at her eyelids.

But...living in a fairy tale and not ready for reality to intrude.

So, she stayed on those heels, stayed plastered to Lucas's chest...and settled in between the pages of a romance novel.

Eventually, though, last call was made and Lucas led her from the club, out to the limo, and into the back.

He didn't sit across from her, not like earlier.

He opened the door, waited for her to clamber in then climbed in after her, lifting her from her seat and plunking her into his lap, wrapping his arms around her.

Breath stolen from the sudden show of strength, from the flare of heat between her legs, it took her a moment to feel his fingers working at her ankles. The clasp of her heel opened and he tugged it off her foot. Then repeated it with her other shoe. Both were tossed onto the seat next to them and then—

"Oh, God," she whispered, head falling back against his shoulder when he began massaging her sore feet.

They'd been in heels all night and were probably sweaty and gross.

But apparently, he didn't mind.

And when his hands slid up, rubbing at the spot where the straps had dug in at her ankles, she moaned softly. Those wonderful hands kept working, not stopping as they began massaging her calves—

Fucking heaven.

He chuckled softly. "Like that, baby?"

Eyes closed, head back against his shoulder, his arms around her, hands gently working at the tension in her body, she knew that she didn't like it.

She fucking *loved* it.

"Mmm," she agreed, breath catching slightly when his hands

moved up a little further, to her knees, to the bottoms of her thighs.

But no further, stopping there and holding her close.

God, he was such a good guy.

"Lucas?"

"Too much?"

Good. Guy.

"No," she whispered.

Still, his hands didn't move, didn't slide higher, just kept lightly stroking patterns on the bottoms of her thighs, raising gooseflesh on her skin and flaring that need in her belly. Especially when she shifted, widening her legs, giving him better access to move those hands higher and felt the hard ridge of his erection against her hip.

"Hmm," he murmured, allowing those fingers to shift higher, grazing her skin so freaking lightly as they trailed along the insides of her thighs.

She widened her legs further.

His hands drifted higher.

"Now?"

"No," she whispered then added, just so it was abundantly clear, "it's not too much."

Another rough chuckle before he trailed those fingers higher, higher, *higher*. Brushing along her thighs, not stopping this time until they met the scrap of fabric covering her pussy.

She gasped, but he didn't ask if she was okay.

Probably because she widened her legs, pressed down onto those fingers, searching out more pressure, wanting the fabric to be out of the way, to just feel his thumb sliding through her slick pussy, to feel his fingers pressing into her.

But he didn't tug the material out of the way.

"Oh!" she gasped when that thumb arrowed in on her clit, pressing against the bundle of nerves in a way that communicated exactly how skilled Mr. Playboy was with a woman's body...and how good it felt to be on the receiving end of all those skills.

His lips found the lobe of her ear, sucking lightly before his tongue flicked out, grazing her skin, sending heat flooding down through her body.

One big, rough hand clasping her thigh. The other cupping her pussy, thumb circling and pressing at her clit, bolts of pleasure zapping through her. Nothing about this felt wrong. It was all right, all perfect, all... So. Fucking. *Good*.

"That's it," he rumbled when her hips bucked, head digging back against his shoulder.

That thumb kept moving, slow and steady, but increasing in pressure.

Increasing the pressure inside *her*.

Breasts tingling, nipples hardening, aching, she rocked against his thumb, already feeling the tension winding and winding and *winding*...ready to explode.

And then he pressed harder.

She bucked, arched, cried out, and thank fuck, but he didn't stop, just kept stroking, kept that pressure exactly as she needed...

And she exploded.

THIRTY

LUCAS

He was hard...and she was snoring.

He grinned when their driver, Rod, opened the door for them and raised his brows, but didn't comment. Lucas ignored the look and just moved, managing to get them both out of the back of the limo without braining her against the frame of the car, without dropping her, and without waking her.

Winning.

"Got her?" Rod asked belatedly, lips curving, gaze taking in far too much of Lucas's woman.

Lucas narrowed his eyes. "Yeah, man, I got her."

The other man glanced away, but not before Lucas saw Rod's lips twitch further.

Fucker.

"Let me grab the rest of your stuff," Rod said and did just that, straightening after a few minutes, arms full, and asking, "Want me to carry it up for you?"

And keep looking at Mads's legs on the way up? Fuck no.

But Lucas just nodded, muttered his thanks.

For one, Lucas didn't have enough hands to carry everything. For another, Rod had been good to them all night, always where he said he'd be, not disappearing or driving his woman around like a fucking maniac.

A smooth ride and circling the block when necessary.

Lucas could control himself.

So long as Rod kept his fucking eyes to himself.

They reached the door to their suite without issue, and Rod was even nice enough to unlock and hold the door for him once Lucas passed him the key.

Probably waiting for a tip.

Which Lucas gave him—and a big fucking one, despite the eyes—after he'd settled Mads in her bed and moved back into the hall to lock up.

He passed over the cash, flicked the lock, the dead bolt, and then started to head back to his room.

But stopped on the threshold.

Mads wasn't under the covers. She might get cold.

Only...tucking her in wasn't the real reason he moved back into Mads's bedroom.

It was...

We don't get to do that anymore.

The dark, barbed instincts inside his mind told him to tuck her in, turn his ass around and sleep in his own bedroom. He didn't deserve to be here, didn't deserve to give in to what he wanted. Not after—

He clenched his teeth together tightly enough to send pain shooting up his jaw.

Reality could come later.

Tonight, he was still living in a fantasy.

And so, when he peeled back the covers to tuck her in...

He tucked himself right in beside her.

———

A phone ringing drew him out of sleep, out of the warm peace of oblivion.

He opened his eyes, blinking against the bright sunshine pouring in through the windows with blinds he hadn't bothered to close—something that was inspiring much regret...

Along with the phone ringing.

Grunting, he reached out, hand scrabbling on the top of the nightstand before he managed to wrap his fingers around his cell and drag it over. Squinting against the bright, he swiped a finger across the screen, lifted it to his ear.

"Yeah?" he rasped.

"And *now* I'm going to kill you."

Ben's voice had the fog of too few hours of sleep clearing, mind focusing, realizing that the weight on his chest wasn't the blankets. It was Mads's head on his shoulder, her arm thrown around his middle. They were still both fully dressed, but when he glanced down, he had an up close and personal look at a gorgeous rack.

His morning wood turned to morning granite.

Not good when the breasts he was staring at belonged to the man on the phone's sister.

"Ben," he muttered. "This isn't a good time to talk about this. Your sister is sleeping—"

The growl had Lucas smacking himself.

"And how would you know that?" Ben snapped. "Unless, I don't know, you fucking took my sister to Vegas and married her—"

"How'd you find out?"

A growl. "Well, *Mr. Playboy*, don't think you've gotten out of the crosshairs of Eva Moreno and her blog just because she's working for the Breakers now. She has her *sources* everywhere and now you've got my sister on her fucking TikTok."

Shit.

Well, that wasn't good.

Or...maybe Mads would think it was cool? He'd break the

news to her later, and if she didn't like it, he'd move hell or high-water to get the video taken down.

"Ben—"

"Save it," Ben gritted out. "There's not one fucking thing you can say that will make this okay. She's my sister, and she's been through hell and—"

"I know," Lucas said. "I know." A breath, keeping the anger out of his tone, his volume down. "I maybe know more than you now, man."

Ben fell silent. Then eventually rasped, "What?"

"We're both very aware this is..." He sighed. "Fast. But we like each other and this works for us."

Ben snorted. "You hated each other all of a month ago."

"Because I was too much of a fucking asshole to see how goddamned perfect she is."

More silence.

But not of the pained or pissed variety.

Lucas decided this was the time to give him the rest. "You know that the social worker said she couldn't take Vivi. This will help, and legal got her in with Bec Darden, who agreed to help her get the charge on her record expunged. That will help too."

Ben sighed. "Fuck, I didn't even think of that."

"She wants to be there for Vivi," Lucas said. "I'm going to make sure that happens."

"I think you could probably do that without marrying her." He exhaled. "Fuck, man. That's my baby sister. I always thought that I'd walk her down the aisle."

"Ben..." Shit. That was...rough, and something *he* hadn't thought about. "It was spur of the moment, a solution that made sense to both of us. I know from the outside it probably seems fucking stupid, but...she's mine," he whispered. "In my heart, I know she's mine."

A jerk against him, and he glanced down, saw that Mads's eyes were open.

And wide.

Then slowly, *slowly* she pushed up from his chest, slipping the phone from his hold. "Ben," she murmured after putting it up to her ear.

There was a long pause as she listened, her eyes never leaving his, the emotion in them telling him that she'd heard far more than his last statement.

"Yeah, big bro," she whispered. "I'm really okay." Her mouth curved. "And as crazy as it probably seems to you and the rest of the outside world, I'm happy."

And still those brown eyes were on his, swimming with emotion that sent his heart pounding.

"Yeah." Another whisper. "Yeah." Her mouth tipped up. "We'll be back to reality soon." A beat. "Soon, being later tonight or tomorrow," she added with a smile. "Yeah. *Yeah.*" Now her eyes rolled and she extended the cell in his direction. "Ben wants to talk to you again."

"Yeah?" Lucas asked, bringing the phone up to his ear as Mads settled back down on his chest.

"Words when you get home," Ben muttered.

Then clicked off before Lucas could reply.

Sighing, he tossed the phone back onto the nightstand, looked up at the woman currently sprawled on his chest. Still flashing him, but he wasn't going to complain.

"Sorry," she whispered.

Lucas tore his eyes from her tits. "I'm not," he told her. "I can handle Ben."

And the fists that would likely be flying his way as soon as he walked into the locker room.

She made a sound that wasn't quite convinced, but then she slid up, lightly pressed her mouth to his. "Thank you," she murmured against his lips. "For what you did." A breath. "For what you said."

He lifted a hand, running a finger lightly up and down her arm. "Nothing to say thanks for."

She shook her head. "Stubborn."

A statement he didn't take the bait on. "You hungry, Peaches?"

Mischief crept into her eyes, and his cock went even harder. That was a good fucking look on her, one that had him imagining her kissing her way down his chest, parting those plump, pink lips and sucking him deep.

He braced, waiting to see what she'd say, what she'd do.

Uncertain if they were going to find somewhere to dance again or order some food or—

Her hand cupped his jaw.

Then slid down his throat, pausing at the center of his shirt and flicked open the top button.

"Yeah, honey"—she bent, flicked out her tongue—"I'm starving."

THIRTY-ONE

MADS

He tasted like sunshine and spice and...*hers*.

His groan, rough and loud, rumbled up through his chest, skating over her skin like the desert's heat blazing down onto her. But it wasn't going to burn her, reduce her to ash. It was as though she were a flower waiting for that exact moment to open her petals, to soak in that sunshine.

Blooming *because* of the blaze.

She flicked open another button, feasting on the skin she exposed, making her way down his chest, opening each fastening and losing herself in the man beneath her.

Not a tendril of fear in place.

Not a moment of not knowing where she was, of worry that she'd freak out, that she'd get hurt or panic or do the wrong thing.

Not with Lucas.

With Lucas...it was right.

His hand went to her hair, not stopping her, just touching her.

She placed a kiss on the hard planes of his pec, slid her fingers along the faint etches of his abdomen, growing deeper with each of his inhalations…which were coming faster the closer she got to the waistband of his slacks. Speaking of which…

"These seem uncomfortable," she murmured, tracing her finger over the button, down along the zipper, feeling his cock twitch beneath the material.

God. It was big. And hard. And…

Her stomach fluttered, thighs quivering, pussy aching.

She slipped a finger beneath the waistband of his slacks, stroking along the velvety head of his cock.

"Mads," he rasped.

She just smiled, flicked open the button, dragged down the zipper.

Freeing his cock.

As she wrapped her hand around him, as his curse hit her ears, as his hips bucked up and his muscles tightened…she wasn't thinking about anything except the desire in her belly and how good his hard cock felt in her fingers and how right it felt being with Lucas like this.

She bent, dipped her head, flicked her tongue over the bead of moisture at the tip, moaning softly as the salty tang settled on her tongue.

His curse was louder.

His muscles went tauter.

That feeling of rightness grew as she parted her lips and slid his cock into her mouth, as his voice reached her ears.

"Jesus, fuck, baby. I—"

The fingers in her hair tightened, and the slight sting on her scalp had her pussy clenching, need growing, wetness slicking the tops of her thighs.

She tightened her hold, sucked him deeper, settled onto the thick expanse of his leg, the hard muscles providing the most delicious type of friction. Up and down, slow and steady and deep. Stroking from base to tip, swallowing as much of him as she could handle.

And repeating the motions.

Over and over again.

Until she was dizzy with desire.

Until she was rocking against him with an urgency that she knew she needed to be careful with, otherwise she was going to come and get distracted and this was going to be over sooner than she wanted.

And she was learning that when it came to Lucas, she wanted *everything.*

His cock in her mouth.

His hands in her hair, on her body.

His lips on her skin, her pussy, her breasts.

But right now, she wanted *this.* Taking this, controlling this, knowing that this hockey player was hers, knowing that she was in charge—

"Ack!" she squeaked and the thought had barely cleared through her mind before she found herself flying through the air, back hitting the mattress, head against the pillows.

Lucas ripping her underwear down her thighs.

Legs spread.

His mouth descending.

And...

Oh, holy shit.

His tongue and lips showed no mercy on her already sensitized clit, rocketing her up toward the peak, readying to launch her off.

"Honey," she murmured. "I—"

A growl. "Hush," he ordered against her pussy. "I'm going to make you come on my tongue and then I'm going to fuck you and you're going to come again."

"I—"

She blinked when he lifted his head, eyes blazing. "You got a problem with that, Peaches?"

"Umm...no?" Actually, that sounded good, really *really* good.

Especially when he dropped his head again and sucked hard on her clit.

"That's what I thought." A nip to the inside of her thigh. "Now lay there and let me eat this glorious pussy."

"I—"

He traced his mouth up along her thigh, over her labia, lapping at her, kissing her, driving her crazy...and then he closed his lips around her clit and sucked again. But this time he did something with his tongue at the same time and...

Not thinking.

She was definitely *not* thinking.

Until he stopped, glanced up at her, lips shining with her desire, beard damp. "That work for you, baby?"

Her hips were undulating, trying to align herself on that *glorious* mouth.

Her mind was a haze of need.

But still the cocky glint in his eyes was the sexiest thing she'd ever seen.

"Yeah," he murmured. "It works for you."

And then he settled in, worked her clit like it was his favorite job, and it wasn't long before her orgasm was on her, wrapping tight around her body, clenching every muscle so...fucking... tight...but just when it seemed impossible to wind tighter, to survive this, pleasure exploded through her, pulsing through her nerves, sending her limbs lax, her mind spinning, her vision hazing.

He saw her through that peak, but as that bliss began to fade, he started back up again.

Tongue and lips working, shooting her toward oblivion a second time and all that much faster because it was like her body knew this man, knew that he was going to bring her something amazing, knew...

He slowly crawled his way up her body, one hand braced by her head, the other playing between her thighs.

And *playing* was exactly what he was doing—keeping her on the edge as he laved across her torso, dragging her dress up as he went, finding the hidden zipper beneath her arm.

That was tugged down, and she was tilted up as he pulled her dress up and over her head.

It flew off somewhere, and he took advantage, attacking her breasts with the same single-minded focus he'd shown her pussy. Driving her fucking insane. Taking her so close to the edge that she felt like she was going to die if she didn't come again.

Then he was on his feet, shoving down his pants and underwear, shrugging out of his unbuttoned shirt.

Retrieving a condom from his wallet.

Rolling it down the hard, glistening length of his cock.

Pausing, his fingers wrapped around the base of his shaft, balls tight, body so fucking unbelievable.

"Okay, Peaches?" he asked softly.

"Inside me," she panted.

He put one knee on the bed. Then the other, crawling over her, cock bobbing. He notched the head at her entrance, paused. "I need to hear the words, baby."

And just like that, the frenzy of need eased. She wasn't turned off, wasn't any less ready to be fucked into oblivion. It was just... emotion was seated at the head of the table as well. Affection for this man, maybe something more, maybe something that would mean *everything*.

And that made it all so much better as she whispered, "I'm okay, honey. I just need you."

Because his expression changed too, and she knew emotion was there for him as well.

Knew it when he slowly slid into her, stretching her until she was almost bursting, until she didn't know where he ended and she began.

Knew it when he rocked gently against her, inching them both toward completion.

Knew it when he held her tight as they both came apart...

And then back together.

Thirty-Two

Lucas

"They don't have any two bedrooms," Mads said, leaning back against the outside wall of the youth center two days later.

They'd been back since yesterday.

Today he'd had practice, and Mads had spoken with the leasing office at her apartment complex about transferring to a two-bedroom.

But apparently, they didn't have any.

Good news was that her record was supposed to be clear in the next couple of days. And she was no longer single, but married to a successful athlete.

Who happened to live in a house with many more than two bedrooms.

Mads sighed and began bundling her hair up on the back of her head, silky strands tumbling down around her nape and her face and making him want to dip his own hand in there, to corral the strands himself...or maybe use them to draw her close so he could kiss that gorgeous mouth. "I'm looking into breaking my lease," she murmured. "I'll see if I can find another apartment, maybe ask Ben to sweet-talk them so they don't gouge me as bad as they can. I just hate that Vivi is stuck at her aunt's. She came by today and she's saying all the right things, but the light in her eyes isn't there. She's not herself."

"Well, you're married to a man who has more than two bedrooms in his house, Peaches. You should just move in with me. She can have her own space. Hell," he added when her brows dragged together, a deep vee forming between them, "*you* could have your own space if you wanted."

Though, he hoped she didn't.

Spending last night holding her, crammed into her queen-sized bed at her apartment, had been the best night of sleep he'd ever had.

"Or," he went on, inspiration striking, "I have a king mattress if you're up for sharing."

That vee didn't go away. "What?" she whispered.

"I mean, we're married, baby. Wouldn't it be weird if you *didn't* move in?" Her eyes went wide. "Keep your apartment, if you want—"

"No," she whispered.

His stomach twisted. "No, what?" he asked carefully. No, she didn't want to move in. Or—

"No," she said again. "I don't need to keep my apartment." She touched his jaw. "Looking forward, right? And it's silly to pay for two places when you have plenty of room."

The knots in his gut relaxed. "Yeah?"

"Yeah," she murmured.

He committed that soft look to memory before focusing. "Should I rally the troops for a moving day?"

"Now?" she asked, brows furrowing again.

He shrugged. "Practice is over. The season hasn't started yet. We're in town. Who knows how soon it'll be before the whole crew is in town and free again?"

Free being a relative term, considering kids and families and other responsibilities.

But the likelihood of having at least a few hands—including her brother's—was great.

"I—" She closed her mouth. Opened it again. Then sighed and shook her head. "Okay," she murmured. Another sigh. "Just...*okay.*"

Lucas grinned, traced his fingers around the shell of her ear. "I'll rally the troops. You finish up here. We'll meet at your apartment in..." He pulled out his cell, glanced at the time. "An hour?"

Teeth pressing into a plump bottom lip.

Then Mads blew out a breath, nodded. "I'll meet you there in an hour."

––––––––

It was more like an hour and a half before everyone showed, but that was okay because it gave him and Mads some time to get ahead on packing up her clothes and all the girly shit in the bathroom.

As for the moving crew, six showed up—Brit, Rome, Coop and Calle, Ben, and Josh.

More than enough to get shit moving and more than enough to make the small apartment feel full to bursting.

Six current and one retired (this being the team's assistant coach and Coop's wife, Calle, and *not* Brit, just for the record) players took up a lot of space. They were all also experienced movers. With players coming and going every season and an ever-expanding Gold family, none of them were strangers to packing up an apartment.

Probably why it took them less than three hours to get the cars, SUV, and truck loaded with Mads's furniture, knickknacks, and clothing.

Something that was made easier because Mads didn't have a lot of stuff.

"You know the way?" he asked after he'd leaned over and buckled her in, holding the frame of the heavy ass door of her rust bucket and thinking that first chance he got, he was going to convince her to let him swap it out for something that didn't look like the engine was going to drop out in the middle of the freeway.

"Yeah, honey," she murmured, reaching out and squeezing his arm. "I have the address on my phone, and"—here her lips twitched—"it's close to Ben's place, so I know where I'm going."

"Closer so your brother can come around the corner and glare at me."

A giggle. "Yeah, probably."

He sighed, brushed his mouth over hers. "Drive safe, and I'll see you over there, Peaches."

They exchanged goodbyes, he closed the door and headed over to Brit's SUV to help her tie off the final couple of ropes securing the furniture they'd stowed in the overhead rack.

"No Stefan today?" he asked as they passed the rope back and forth, pulling it taut and then tossing it back.

Brit missed the length of nylon, stepping out of the door frame and bending down to snatch it up. "He's busy," she said softly, standing back up onto the metal step and winding the rope through the rack before tossing it back.

"He's been busy a lot lately," Lucas said, intending to add a teasing remark about Roxie—their adopted daughter—keeping them running.

But his comment didn't make Brit laugh and respond how the other guys would have, sharing their kids' busy schedules, complaining about the multitude of extracurriculars Roxie was in. Instead, her face fell and she avoided eye contact with him. Which sent alarm bells blaring through his mind.

"Brit," he began.

"You're going to treat Mads right," she said firmly, reaching over and extending her hand, signaling for the rope.

He passed it back, wavering about what to say next.

Brit didn't give him the chance. "If you don't, it's going to make trouble in the locker room, and it's early in the season. We need to have our heads straight, need to be focusing on coming together instead of pulling apart."

"I'll give her everything she deserves." More. He'd give her the fucking world if it was within his ability.

"Even love?"

His head jerked back to Brit, her tone not normal, not bubbly, not *Brit*. It was...jaded, sharp.

And it was clear that she interpreted his processing her tone, him not immediately responding with the affirmative of something it wasn't.

Because love?

Mads already had his.

She just didn't know it yet.

He was saving that for a moment that wasn't filled with trauma and worry and angst. A time when it was just them and he could make it clear his heart was hers.

"Yeah," Brit whispered, shaking her head as she secured the final length of rope then hopping down, cutting off his view of her face.

But not before he saw the stark expression, the pain in those chocolate brown eyes.

Her next words barely reached his ears. "That's what I thought."

"Brit—"

He didn't finish because she was already climbing into the SUV, slamming the driver's side door, turning on the engine, and not looking at him as she pulled away from the curb.

Leaving him watching the SUV disappear into the distance and wondering about love...

And if Brit still had it.

Thirty-Three

MADS

"Holy shit," she panted, dropping her head onto his shoulder. "Eva Moreno is fucking right."

His breaths were coming equally as rapid as he carefully lowered her feet to the ground, their celebration of their first night in his house together having come to a very pleasurable conclusion.

It was morning, the sun was shining brightly.

And she'd spent the third night of her life in Lucas's arms...

Feeling safe and protected and...*right*.

He sighed and shook his head, holding her hips steady when her legs threatened to give way—because the orgasm this man had just given her had turned them to jelly. "You're supposed to hate the fact you're on her TikTok."

It was wild.

It was a fantasy.

But Mads was finally accepting that her hockey player was giving her a life that was better than any she could have ever dreamed of.

So, she'd settled on being excited about the TikTok.

"Well, Mr. Playboy"—he scowled—"I'm on the receiving end of all you've learned with *all* of your *extensive* experience and—*eek!*"

He growled and tossed her on the bed. "I'll show you *extensive* experience."

Yeah, okay, she didn't mind that threat.

Especially when it had his mouth hitting hers, giving her a scorching kiss that had her lost in need, in this man, in his hands sliding along her body, cupping her breasts, rolling her nipples with just the right amount of pressure.

Definitely didn't mind when he released her mouth and kissed his way down along her torso, parting her legs in a smooth move.

And spending of some quality time with her pussy.

"Oh, God!" she moaned, arching back, grinding against his mouth, seeking out the orgasm that was. Just. Right. There.

She came, pleasure cascading through her.

Pleasure that was still peaking as he rolled on a condom, spread her legs, and stroked inside, sparking her into another orgasm or maybe just extending the one already flowing through her. Either way, it was fucking glorious and she held on to big broad shoulders, reveling in the sensations, in the wonder of being here, like this. With a man. With *this* man, and feeling safer and more protected and more comfortable than she'd ever been.

Not because he'd apologized or because he'd bought her a pretty dress.

But because he'd shown her who he was and...she liked it.

A lot.

And he saw her as *her*.

Not an addict. Not a fucked-up person who'd done fucked-up things. And when she struggled to remember she was more than that, he stepped in and reminded her.

She could be *more*.

———

A brush of his lips over hers had her grunting, her body limp and eyelids heavy from his *extensive* experience. "You've killed me."

He chuckled. "I've got to get to the rink."

"How are you still walking?"

"Strong legs, Peaches." He kissed her forehead. "Rest," he murmured. "But make sure you call Donna."

Her eyes flew open.

Shit. She'd been so wrapped up in the fact that sex was... fucking great and all-encompassing and could mean something, so wrapped up in this fairy tale and this man and liking the person she was when they were together...that she'd forgotten.

Forgot Vivi.

Shit.

She was a bad person—

No.

Just. Fucking. Stop.

She was allowed this moment of joy, the crazy, wild ride that was making her happy. She deserved good things.

She deserved *everything.*

She wanted to tattoo that on her soul. She wanted to show Vivi the same—because that girl was awesome and she deserved everything too and—

Mads sat up, saw that Lucas was studying her, watching her closely as she worked through that.

Watching her *patiently.*

"Good," he murmured, clearly seeing she'd come to the conclusion—to the *right* conclusion. "Good, Peaches."

She took his hand. "We deserve good things," she whispered. "You, me, *and* Vivi."

His big chest expanded on an inhale. He held it for a moment then released it. "Yeah, baby, we do."

"I'll call Donna," she said.

"Vivi doesn't like the guest room, she can have her pick of the others," he told her. "Furniture too. She can use what's there or we can get her new stuff."

"Lucas," Mads murmured.

"*We* deserve good things, remember? You, me, *and* Vivi."

Her eyes started stinging, but God, so much heavy, so much dark in her past. She wanted to stay in the light. So, she did, dug her toes into the proverbial hot sand, let the rays of the sun warm her...and she embraced this moment, this man.

This life.

Touching his jaw, she nodded. "Vivi's a teenage girl"—her mouth quirked—"I'm sure shopping is on the agenda."

A nod. "I'll leave my card on the counter. Use that to buy her a new comforter and shit." Her heart rolled over in her chest, love for this man exploding through her. He started to stand, paused. "And I'll see about getting her a ticket if she wants to come to the game tonight. You mind missing out on your seat?"

Another roll in her chest, pulse pounding.

Love burning through her veins.

"I know the guy who sits next to me," she murmured. "I'll see if he wants to sell his ticket. I know weekday games are tough for him to go to."

"It's the home opener," Lucas said. "He might not want—"

"Then we'll watch from home or from different seats."

"Or the family suite," he said softly.

Mads's lungs expanded in a rush, but she just nodded. "Yeah," she whispered. "Or we'll watch from the family suite."

Because Vivi would need that—the big, boisterous, nosy Gold crew, who embraced with open arms and resembled the mafia in many ways, as Mads had experienced. Once in, there were no outs. Vivi needed those types of people at her back.

"Text me and let me know what's up, yeah?"

She nodded.

He touched her cheek, face softening. "Thanks for marrying me."

Her heart pulsed, and she covered his hand with her own, embracing the light. "You look hot in that suit."

They'd been soft and sweet, spicy and bone-meltingly plea-surable.

Now she got to watch him throw his head back and laugh, loud and long.

And she got to taste that laugh on her tongue.

It was perfection.

And then, clad in that gorgeous fucking suit, his ass—God, hockey players had the best asses—he straightened and headed for the door.

"I'll see you after the game, Peaches."

————

"Hey," she said, moving to sit next to Vivi.

The girl was perched on one of the benches in the youth center, shaded beneath an old oak tree that sat in the middle of the garden some of the kids liked to work on. Mostly flowers, but a few boxes with vegetables they were trying to grow with varying success.

Vivi glanced up from the book in her lap. "Hey."

"What are you reading?"

She held up the book so Mads could see the cover. It was one she'd seen all over TikTok. "Any good?"

Vivi shrugged. "Yeah, it's okay."

"How are things with your aunt?"

Vivi went stiff, but only for a fraction of a second before she shrugged. "It's fine."

"*Fine,* fine?" Mads asked. "Or fine as in you don't want me to worry so you'll suck it up, keep your mouth closed and pretend everything is good."

Vivi stilled, but again, only for a second before she shrugged. "Everything's fine, as in *fine,* and you don't need to worry."

Such a sweet liar.

"Is she hurting you?" Because she might be planning on

having Vivi with her, but if Vivi's aunt had done something to harm her, Mads was going to rain down fire.

Vivi turned her head, holding Mads's eyes for the first time that day. "No. She's a raging bitch and never lets me forget that she's *doing me a favor* by taking me in, but she's not the worst place I've stayed."

"Nick?" Mads asked.

Vivi turned away, tone revealing far too much even though her words were almost robotic. "My mom is shit at picking men. Nick is an asshole who likes to use his fists, but he's not the worst."

Fuck.

Mads *had* to get her to agree to come live with her and Lucas.

"Anyway, there's food and internet." A bland shrug. "And it's not long before I turn eighteen."

Three years yet.

That was an eternity when someone was in hell.

"And Pascal gave me his number," Vivi told her. "He said if things get really bad to call him and he'd come."

Of course he had. Because Pascal was the shit.

"Good," she murmured. "You can rely on him."

Vivi's gaze came to Mads's. "Yeah." Then she dropped her eyes down to her book. "So, you don't have to worry about me. You and Lucas can do your thing and—"

Damn, gossip traveled fast.

Through the Gold.

Through the youth center.

And through TikTok, she supposed.

That explained why Mads had needed to seek the girl out instead of Vivi joining her for their usual time together.

"I talked to Donna today."

At the mention of the social worker's name, Vivi stilled again.

Mads gave her the rest of it. "Lucas and I made things official because it helped smooth over some obstacles that meant you couldn't stay with me."

Vivi's head shot up.

"I moved into his house over the weekend," she said softly. "He's got plenty of bedrooms, and you can have your pick."

Vivi's lips parted.

Mads reached over, squeezed her hand. "Donna will go to bat for us if you want to leave your aunt's and move in with Lucas and me."

Vivi started shaking her head. "He wouldn't want to—"

"Honey," she said, taking Vivi's hand. "Lucas and I wouldn't even be a thing if not for you."

"I—"

She squeezed lightly. "He and I needed a push to see the good that was in front of us. I was worried about you. He stepped in and offered to help me track you down"—she narrowed her eyes, silently warning the girl to not pull that shit again—"In doing that, he helped me see that I, that *we* deserve way more than we think we do."

Vivi's fingers convulsed inside Mads's.

"So, yeah, Lucas is all in for me and for you—" She chuckled at Vivi's expression, a combination of disbelief and shock and maybe more than a little dash of hope. "He invited you to the hockey game tonight and even left his credit card in case you wanted to go shopping for *a new comforter and shit*. His words," she added lightly and was relieved to see the corners of Vivi's mouth turn up. "So, yeah, Viv, Lucas and I are doing our thing, but we also want to do it with you."

Those fingers twitched again.

"So, what do you say, honey? Wanna go buy a new comforter and shit and then go to your first Gold hockey game?"

Vivi's fingers tightened.

And then the girl smiled.

It was fucking beautiful.

Thirty-Four

He skated by the glass, gaze flicking up to the stands, seeing that Mads and Olivia were sitting side by side. Not in her normal seat, but one section over, tickets from the team's pool.

Not watching from the family suite because Mads thought that might be too overwhelming.

Baby steps.

But baby steps had involved Donna and Bec lighting a fire under a judge's ass, Mads and Vivi packing up her things and moving them into one of the spare bedrooms in his house.

Then going shopping for a new comforter.

And towels. And shams—whatever the fuck those were. And a few knickknacks.

Mads taking him at his word, giving Vivi everything.

He smiled up at the woman who owned his heart, then turned and waved at Vivi, who gave him a small smile and an awkward wave. But her eyes held wariness.

Still taking his measure.

That was fine.

He'd get there.

"So, there *is* a limit to your superpowers?" Rome said, bending and snagging a puck from the ice, tossing it into the gaggle of kids standing—and pounding—on the other side of the glass. "And it's teenage girls?"

"Rude," Lucas muttered, bending for another puck and tossing it over the boards as well. "We barely know each other from the youth center, but we'll get there. I'll win her over."

Rome paused, studied his face.

"What?"

His teammate's voice sounded surprised. "I actually think you're right."

Lucas glared.

Rome grinned and shook his head, lifting his gloved hands, palms out in surrender, stick swinging around like a fucking projectile. "Look, man, you were a fucking dick to her, and yeah, I get that you've turned that shit around, but that was a *big* turn around, and I'd be lying if I said I wasn't shocked that Mads's in the stands looking that happy. Almost as shocked as you announcing to the locker room that Vivi is moving in with you both and to make sure the girl feels welcome."

Okay, yeah, Lucas had made some threats in the locker room.

Vivi needed the team, and he didn't want anyone fucking it up.

"They're mine," he muttered.

Those palms lifted again. "I'm not debating that."

Lucas dodged again.

"I'm just experiencing whiplash," his teammate said.

"Maybe you should *experience* some fucking hockey and then help me make sure that Vivi finds a home with the team."

Rome dropped his hands and the blade of his stick hit the ice with a soft *crack*. "Fair enough."

Then the fucker skated away.

Though he paused, smirked at Lucas over his shoulder. "I'm thinking that you should *experience some hockey* too."

Said just as the buzzer rang, signaling it was time for them to get their asses back to the locker room.

An ice cut.

The national anthem.

Then some fucking hockey.

A whistle had him glancing up at the stands...at Mads.

Who mouthed, "Focus."

Lucas saluted and turned for the bench, through which was the exit to the locker room, and as he skated across the ice, he did it grinning.

Because Mads was giving him playing advice now.

And he fucking loved it.

———

Much later, after the game had finished, the crowd happy because their team had won their first game of the season, he moved quietly into his house.

Feeling weird, but in a good way.

Because this was the first time since he'd made it into the NHL that he came home to a house full of people who belonged to him.

Mads.

Vivi.

Yeah, he was going to watch out for his girls.

Starting by being as quiet as possible as he could be coming in after midnight.

He caught the door before it could slam closed, moving into the kitchen and flicking on the under-cabinet lights. He needed to eat something healthy that fit in with his meal plan and wouldn't leave him ravenous in the morning and—

A gasp had him freezing.

He looked over, saw Vivi standing in the open fridge, face stark, the milk carton she'd been about to pull out quickly stashed back on the shelf. "I'm sorry," she said softly. "I-I-I—" She swallowed hard and then seemed to brace herself for a fortifying breath. "I was hungry and—"

His gaze flicked to the bowl on the counter, the box of sugary cereal and he knew that Mads was taking care of Vivi.

But he also knew that Vivi didn't trust him.

She'd taken a leap moving in with a man she barely knew, after a lifetime of living with untrustworthy people, after a lifetime of being fucked over by everyone...except Mads.

He moved to her, slow and steady, and hating that she braced herself again.

But he knew he could get them through to the other side of this, so he kept moving, slowly, carefully, until he was close enough to reach beyond Vivi, to snag the milk carton back out, to carry it to the counter and set it next to the bowl and box of cereal.

"Spoons are here," he murmured, opening a drawer in the island and placing one of the silver utensils on the counter next to the midnight snack fixings. "There's a pad of paper and pen next to the fridge for groceries. If there's something that you want and it's not here, write it down and I'll make sure it lands on the next grocery order."

She blinked.

"And anything in these cupboards, in the fridge, freezer, or pantry are yours. Eat your fill and don't apologize, and don't worry that anyone's going to get mad because you finish something off. This is your home for as long as you want it to be."

Another slow blink.

"Except the alcohol," he said, realizing that was in the fridge and the cupboard next to it, that it was the one thing she couldn't have. "That'll have to wait until you're twenty-one."

Her blinking had returned to normal, but now her mouth dropped open.

Then closed.

Then opened again.

And he had the sense that she needed some time to process the interaction.

"Eat your cereal," he murmured, knowing *his* midnight snack could wait. "I'll see you in the morning, yeah?"

He watched her swallow. Once. Twice.

Then she nodded, whispered, "See you in the morning."

He walked out of the kitchen, turned down the hall, ready to be out of this suit, ready to see and hold and maybe fuck Mads if he could tempt her to do it in the bathroom so they didn't scar the teen who had joined their newly formed family (whether or not she understood that yet). But before he made it to the stairs, he saw Mads standing about halfway down.

Their gazes locked and his heart started pounding.

Her eyes glimmered, the emotion in the deep brown depths sending his pulse shooting even faster through his veins.

Her lungs hitched and then he was moving again, moving faster.

Cupping her jaw.

Wiping away the tears that clung to her bottom lashes.

"Peaches," he whispered.

Her hand covered his, their faces aligned with her being on the step above the one he'd paused on. Which meant he was staring right into those damp brown eyes, knowing she must have overheard him in the kitchen with Vivi, seeing how much it meant to her.

He knew already.

Because it was important to him too.

But seeing that joy on her face hit him hard and deep and—

"I love you," she whispered.

He'd been thinking the same, had the words on his tongue, but had been holding them back because...well, because of everything.

Hearing them from her?

Fuck, holding back wasn't even an option.

"Baby," he whispered. "I love you too."

Her eyes welled again, and she exhaled. "We've lost our goddamned minds." Still whispering, but this time with a layer of amusement.

Unable to stand there with her a step away, his palm on her cheek, he dipped down, wrapped his arms around her thighs, and lifted her up and over his shoulder into a fireman's hold. "Yeah, Peaches, we've lost our minds." He slid his hand up, cupped one lush cheek, hearing her breath catch. "But we're doing it together, so it's fucking great."

Her body went slack in his hold.

Then she laughed quietly and said, "Yeah, honey, it sure is."

THIRTY-FIVE

MADS

Being a friend-slash-responsible adult-slash-surrogate parent to a teenager wasn't for the faint of heart.

Especially one who'd been through the wringer like Vivi had.

It wasn't even that she was rude or snappy or hormonal—Vivi was beyond polite, the glimpses of sass she'd given Mads at the youth center few and far between.

The girl was on edge, probably worried that Mads and Lucas would pull the plug on the living arrangement, send her back to her aunt's or worse, she'd end up with her mom and in Nick's crosshairs.

Nick, who hadn't shown his face.

But he was good at that, good at hiding in the shadows before he popped out like the fucking gremlin he was to fuck with shit.

Vivi wasn't going back to that.

She just didn't trust that truth yet.

So, patience and time and trying not to acknowledge the tenseness that wasn't getting better, even with two weeks under her belt living at Lucas's place.

Mads paused.

Thought about the last part of that sentence.

Lucas's place.

She called it that in her head and out loud...to Vivi.

So yeah, that couldn't be helping and needed to change. Not just for Vivi but for herself too. They were both *home* here, and of course they needed time to settle, but if she was throwing up barriers, even in her own head, it wasn't going to help.

All that therapy was helping.

Look at her go, so well adjusted.

Grinning, she pushed open the door from the garage. "Hey, Viv!" she called, "Georgia sent peanut butter bars."

Vivi glanced up from where she was doing her homework at the island, and her wrinkled nose had Mads giggling.

"If you can believe it," she said. "They're not as bad as her chocolate chip cookies."

"Well, considering that her chocolate chip cookies made me want to wash my mouth out with soap, that's saying something."

She set the bag on the counter next to Vivi's elbow, peered over her shoulder and her mind immediately went fuzzy just glancing at the array of complicated math equations littering the page. Good God, was that what they made kids do these days?

"Why are you reading in a foreign language when you're supposed to be doing math?"

Vivi giggled, and hearing her girl laugh was pretty much the best sound in the world. "It's calculus, Mads."

"Isn't that, like, a college course?"

"Maybe in the caveman days," Vivi said.

"And that's—what—inferring that *I'm* a caveman—or cave-woman, anyway?"

Vivi shrugged, mouth curving up. "I mean, *I* didn't say it."

"Just for that," Mads teased, "I'm going to make you eat a peanut butter bar and tell Georgia how much you liked them, so the next time you go over with me, she'll make you eat an entire pan of them."

"Evil."

Mads just buffed her knuckles on her shoulders and grinned. Though she did manage to get down to business. Lucas was at the gym with Rome and a few of the other guys. He'd be home soon and hungry...and she was starving, considering that she'd spent the last couple of hours going through Georgia's cabinets and dusting several hundred porcelain dolls.

She shuddered.

Those beady eyes would stay with her for a good long time.

"You hungry?" she asked instead of sharing her horror of the porcelain dolls.

"Is it going to be more of that green stuff that Lucas has to eat?" Vivi countered, wrinkling her nose and giving Mads a glimpse of sass.

And hell if that wasn't better than the giggle.

Because it was the Vivi of old.

"It's not a Cheat Day," Mads said, leaning into that nose wrinkle. "So, while there will be green stuff, Lily shared the recipe, and she swears it tastes really good."

Vivi doubled down on the wrinkled nose.

"Lily and Will are like you. Not fans of green stuff or tofu or anything that resembles healthy food." Not entirely true, but she was trying to sell Vivi on this venture into Lucas's healthy meal plan...and maybe eating something that wasn't comprised solely of corn syrup and green food dye. "And they both love it."

That nose wrinkle didn't go away.

"And we can always order pizza and make Lucas feel jealous if it's terrible. Deal?"

Vivi's nose smoothed out and she nodded. "Deal."

They fist-bumped, and Mads had just gone to the fridge to get out the ingredients when the doorbell rang.

Vivi started to get up, but Mads caught her shoulder. "I'll get it. You keep melting your brain with calculus."

Another giggle that settled in her belly.

Which was why she was smiling when she opened the door.

She was not ready to see the woman on the other side. Not prepared. Not *fucking ready.*

For her mother to be standing on the porch.

She didn't talk to the woman standing in front of her any more than necessary. There were some things that couldn't be undone in Mads's opinion, couldn't be erased, and the fact that her mother hadn't been much of one for her entire life, not to mention hadn't initially believed Mads when she'd gone to her about Bill...

No.

She didn't want to see her mother.

Her healthy, sober, no- manipulating-everyone-in-her-life-to-get-her-next-fix self saw this woman for what she was.

Ben could make his peace with her, however stilted and distant it was.

Mads could be polite for the sake of family, for the sake of her nephews having more people in their lives who loved them.

But she didn't want...*this.*

Her mother showing up on Lucas's—on *her*—doorstep out of the blue.

Her mom's eyes flicked down to Mads's hand—to Mads's *left* hand—then back up. "It's true."

Yeah, she didn't want to do this, not with Vivi in the kitchen and her mind determined to be moving forward.

"I'm sorry, Mom," Mads said softly. "This isn't a good time." She reached for the door, intending to close it, which was rude, yes, but also all the politeness she could summon.

But her mother proved that politeness wasn't on the agenda.

"Didn't take you long to find your way to the top, did it?" A flick of her gaze behind Mads, presumably taking in the entry of Lucas's house, which was more than a little grand with a wide staircase. "Did you use what you learned on the street?"

She gasped, staggering back a step. "Did you seriously just say that to me?"

Her mom's chin came up. "This is quite a house." Her eyes flicked down again. "And that's quite a ring."

Thirty seconds with her mother, and Mads felt...dirty.

Worse than when she fucked a man because he let her have some pills, worse than selling the broach that belonged to Georgia's grandmother, worse than devastating her brother with her words, her actions.

Because this was attacking something she'd only just accepted could be hers. This was sinking claws into her heart and tearing it to shreds.

This was—

"Or is he a user too and you get fucked up together?"

"Shut up!"

Mads jerked, sliding out of the pained haze that had begun to intrude, to cling to the edges of her mind, to make that deep, buried part of herself long to make this all go away.

To not feel anything.

To seek out blissful numbness.

But Vivi's voice had her snapping out of that, whirling and seeing the girl running toward her. "Shut up!" she said again, wrapping her arm around Mads's middle and hugging her close. "Don't talk to her like that."

Her sweet girl.

God, Vivi was killing her.

And her mother didn't see the show of solidarity as anything but a nuisance. Her expression went pure sneer.

"And who's *this* little bitch?"

THIRTY-SIX

LUCAS

He came in through the back door, breathing heavy, sweat beading down his back, muscles screaming, mind on all the tape he needed to review before their game tomorrow.

It took a minute for him to process that no one was in the kitchen.

Vivi's books were on the island, and the fridge door was open and beeping.

His instincts prickled.

He had run over to finish his workout, jogging from Ben's house—well, really from Ben's home gym—and, at the request of Marcus and Sam, his mission was to either talk the girls into dinner at their house or to con their way into dinner here. Lucas didn't care either way, but he'd left his car at Ben's, already knowing what Mads's answer would be.

A night with her nephews trumped almost everything.

Even though she'd worked all day and had spent a couple of hours helping Georgia afterward.

Vivi was the wild card.

But considering how amenable she'd been in the couple of weeks since she and Mads had moved in, he figured she'd take Mads's lead.

"Shut up! Don't talk to her like that."

His instincts went into overdrive at the sound of Vivi's voice echoing into the room, and he ran through the kitchen, ignoring the beeping from the fridge as he moved into the hall.

And saw what was happening at the front door.

Ben and Mads's mom, Lydia, standing in the opening.

Vivi with her arm around Mads's waist.

And Mads bent over, shoulders hunched, hips tucked in. Like she got fucking punched. Like she was trying to curl into a fucking protective ball.

He reached into his pocket, pulled out his cell, and called Ben.

His teammate answered on the first ring. "You heading here—?"

"Get your ass over here," Lucas snapped. "Now."

"Wh—"

But Lucas was already hanging up, tossing his cell on the narrow table he kept in the hall as a landing pad for all his shit, and he strode across the room.

The clatter drew the attention of the women.

And the look on Mads's face as she turned to face him had him considering murder.

"Vivi," he said, and it was a fucking struggle to keep his tone neutral. "Will you take Mads into the kitchen?"

Vivi's eyes were wide, but she nodded, started guiding Mads back from the door.

Lydia snorted, disdain in her eyes as she glanced at her daughter. "Always pretending to be so fragile. You're pathetic."

Mads flinched.

And Lucas had *had* it.

"Vivi?"

She might only be fifteen, but Vivi got it, taking Mads's arm, drawing her back, leading her toward the kitchen.

Only the moment that she and Vivi started to move by him, their eyes locked and their fingers brushed and...Mads's expression cleared. He saw it in an instant, and the relief in his stomach hit so hard that he almost lost his breath.

While he was processing that, she whirled around, dislodging Vivi's arm and marching over to her mom.

"How dare you?" she hissed, bending and getting into her mother's face. "How *dare* you? *You* who fucked up Ben's and my lives—"

"Nice language in front of the kid," Lydia said with a sneer.

Mads froze, glanced back over her shoulder, guilt on her face.

"Yeah, exactly. I used to blame myself for your actions." Lydia huffed. "Used to accept the blame you settled on my shoulders. But you're a grown-up now, and it's still the same thing. *I* was the one who was hurt, and you and your brother never saw things my way after your father left."

"Ben killed himself to make enough money as a freaking eight-year-old so we could share a loaf of bread and a jar of peanut butter."

Vivi sucked in a breath.

Lucas reached out, took her hand.

Nodded slightly when she clutched his fingers hard enough to make his bones protest.

"And you didn't see that, didn't make sure you were a parent for us. Didn't do anything but pretend to be a good mother when in reality you were anything but."

"How dare you?" Lydia snapped.

Mads snorted and shook her head, and he inched closer, keeping Vivi behind him while he positioned himself to intervene if Lydia took things physical.

Because Mads's mother's hands were tense at her sides, fingers curled like she was ready to claw her daughter's eyes out.

"You just had to fuck a hockey player, didn't you? Had to weasel your way in with your brother and make it all about you.

Again." She huffed out a breath. "It's always about poor Mads or poor, strong Mads, or poor, strong, fucked-up Mads."

He took a step closer, Vivi right at his back, but neither of them got the chance to say anything as Mads tabled her rage and her hurt, and her steel came out.

The quiet, unbreakable strength.

"You mean nothing to me. You are part of my past," Mads said. "But there is absolutely no way that you will be part of my future."

Lydia's eyes went wide.

Probably because Mads's tone left no room for commentary.

"I could have forgiven you for everything that happened if you actually cared about me and not how it reflected on you. Hell, I would have begged *you* for forgiveness for my actions if I wasn't running from the burdens you settled so heavily on my shoulders, if you hadn't treated Ben like you did, if you weren't here right now, spitting venom and trying to make me small again." Mads shook her head. "But I'm done. I'm not going to allow you to be part of my future."

"You—"

"I'm not either."

The male voice had Lydia swiveling around, Mads jumping, Lucas's gaze going to the walkway, seeing Ben taking the last two steps that led onto the porch.

"Benny."

Ben moved by his mom, ignoring her pleading intonation of his name and looked between Lucas, Vivi, and Mads. "You guys okay?"

"You either get her the hell out of here," Lucas said because Mads was definitely not okay, "or I will." He could stand back and let Mads show her strength, but he couldn't stand there on his fucking heels forever, not doing anything while her mother spit out vitriol.

It reminded him too much of being a kid, standing and taking the abuse.

No, he wouldn't let that happen to Mads.

"Benny!"

Ben snorted. "Seriously? I let you back into my life, and this is the bullshi—" He slanted a glance over his shoulder at Vivi and blew out a breath, tone still frosty, but a lot more controlled. "After everything, after *everything* we've all been through, for you to come here and act like this, to say that stuff to my sister, my baby fuck—my *baby sister*...no freaking way—"

"Ben?"

He stopped, glanced at his sister.

"I've got this."

Ben clenched his jaw, a muscle flexing in his cheek, but he shifted, moved to stand next to Vivi and Lucas. Taking her back but clearly wanting to be in between Mads and the world.

Considering that Lucas was in the middle of that very same battle, he had sympathy.

But he was still approximately one second away from kicking that bitch out of his house.

"You are no one to me," Mads said. "Not *ever* again. And I don't want to see you again. Not now. Not a month from now. Not a fucking decade from now. And if you try to hurt Ben or me or Jordyn or Marcus or I or Vivi or Lucas, or *anyone* that I love again"—Vivi inhaled next to him, her hand convulsing around Lucas's—"I swear I will find you and make you pay."

Then she placed her hand in the middle of her mom's chest and started walking forward, not so much shoving as corralling her out the front door.

And slamming it shut.

And flicking the lock.

And turning to them.

"I'm so sorry—"

"Don't." Lucas squeezed Vivi's hand, letting her know silently that he was there before he released it and stepped toward Mads, brushing his knuckles over her cheek. "I am so *fucking* proud of you."

Mads exhaled. "I didn't mess up."

"You were fucking incredible, Peaches."

She exhaled. "This should hurt more," she whispered. "But I only feel...relieved."

"No, it shouldn't," Vivi said, coming close, and Mads wrapped her arm around her. "You *should* feel relieved. You don't need people like her in your life. You're a good person, Mads, and she's—she's..."

"Gone for good," Ben finished.

Mads closed her eyes, sighed, and nodded. "I'm sorry that you had to see that, Viv. You—"

"I'm not," Viv said. "You kicked ass." She grinned. "Which is a heck of a lot better than calculus." Then she rose on tiptoe, pressed a kiss to Mads's cheek, dropped to her heels, and disappeared into the kitchen, unaffected like only a teenager could be.

"You good?" Lucas asked softly once she'd gone.

"No," Mads whispered, turning into the circle of his arms, holding him tight. "But I will be. For the first time, I truly know I will be."

He hugged her back, locked eyes with Ben, and his teammate slipped out the door.

Lucas knew he was making sure that Lydia left and stayed gone.

Long minutes passed and Ben didn't come back in, later sending a text saying that he'd placated the boys with the promise of dinner another night.

Because her brother got it.

Tonight, Mads needed to be with the little family she was building.

And Lucas needed it too.

THIRTY-SEVEN

MADS

"Mads?"

She glanced up from where she was digging and smiled when Vivi came out. "Yeah, Vivs?"

"Can you help me with—?" Vivi frowned, stopping a few feet away. "What are you doing?"

She patted the dirt down over the little hole she'd dug, making sure not to cover the slender green shoot she'd been carefully growing these last weeks. "Planting."

That frown deepened. "*That's* what you're planting?"

She'd slowly been coaxing a tendril of a plant out from the peach pit she'd saved. The one from her first morning at their house, the first moment she'd truly felt at home here. Now weeks had passed and the pit had split open, the seed inside showing signs that it was time to hit the dirt.

It seemed like kismet that it was the right time of year to plant the seed.

And it was sunny today, the clouds broken up with stripes of bright blue sky and...

It just seemed like the right time to be sitting in her back yard, hands in the dirt, planting the seeds of something that would take years to grow strong, to bloom, to bear fruit.

Like her.

Like Lucas.

She smiled and gave the ground one more pat before pushing up to her feet and brushing her hands on her jeans. "What'd you need help with?"

"Oh." Vivi glanced from the shoot up at Mads and seemed to lose her courage. "Never mind. You're busy and—"

"Vivi."

"You're busy," she whispered.

"I'm planting a single seed. It's not exactly labor intensive." Mads gestured at the ground. "And something that's done now."

"Oh. Right."

"So. What'd you need help with? Anything, honey," she added when Vivi hesitated, nibbling at her bottom lip.

"Can you read through the story I wrote?"

A small, scared question.

One followed up immediately by rushed words. "It's just a short one and it's not important. My English teacher just said that sometimes it helps to have other people read—" She went back to nibbling at her lip.

"I'd love to, hun," Mads said, putting her out of her misery. "Want to go get it and I'll wash my hands?"

More nibbling.

But this time it was accompanied by a yawn.

"Yeah, okay."

When Vivi didn't immediately move, Mads laced their arms together, started drawing her kiddo toward the house. Thankfully, that seemed to snap Vivi out of her fog and when they reached the kitchen, she peeled off for her room...and presumably that story.

Mads went to the sink, washed up, and was drying her hands when Vivi came back in with a notebook.

For a second, she thought Vivi would chicken out.

But then she seemed to force herself to move, to hand Mads the notebook. "It's just that page and the next three."

Just.

Mads internally shook her head. But since her sweet girl was clearly nervous, she kept anything that might be construed as negative under lock and key. "Okay, hun," she said evenly, taking the notebook to the table and sitting down.

"I—"

Mads paused. "Do you want to work on it some more before I read it?"

Silence.

And she expected Vivi to take her up on that out.

But her kiddo was made of sterner stuff. She sucked in a breath, straightened her shoulders, and lifted her chin. "No," she said. "I want you to read it now."

Mads nodded.

And started reading.

And...was immediately swept away into another world. There was intrigue and mystery and a dash of romance. A kickass heroine and a swoony hero and it was all in three front-and-back pages.

She devoured—absolutely *devoured*—the story, and when she got to the end, heart pounding, mind wanting more, she looked up to see that Vivi was standing there, nibbling on that lip again.

"Come here, honey," Mads said softly, closing the notebook and patting the seat next to her.

Vivi moved slowly, creeping over to the chair, slowly lowering herself into it.

"This—"

Viv sucked in another breath.

"—is *incredible.*"

Vivi had been looking at her hands, but Mads's sentence had her head shooting up, air hissing out. "What?"

"Honey"—she took her hand—"you are supremely talented."

"I—"

"Calculus. Acing your history test. Winning over Sam and Marcus and countless other kids at the center. Eating food that's dyed a fluorescent green—"

That had Vivi unsticking, lips tipping up just at the corners.

So Mads squeezed her hand again, adding when she knew now that the girl would actually hear it, "And writing, honey. You're really, *really* good at writing."

A shaky breath.

But Vivi's eyes didn't slide away and she didn't make a self-deprecating comment. She just nodded and murmured, "I really like doing it. I think—" She braced herself. "I think that I might want to do it as a career."

"Then we're going to the stationery store and getting you a proper notebook and pens—"

They both jerked, hands falling apart, gazes going behind them...

To where Lucas was leaning against the wall.

As they watched, he pushed off the wall and moved to the pad of paper next to the fridge, picking up the pen he always left with it. "Notebooks," he muttered, almost to himself, as he wrote. "Pens and pencils. And a laptop. She needs a good computer, something that won't shut down on her and make her lose her work." He paused, tapped the pen to his lips then finally looked back at them. "What else does a writer need?"

Vivi unstuck first. "I don't need—"

"A desk," he said, turning back to the pad. "You should already have one. And a good chair. And a lamp, in case you need more light. Post-Its. Index cards. A bulletin board for ideas—"

"Mads," Vivi whispered.

She blinked, managed to pull herself back together as she turned away from Lucas and his continued list-making. He was still in his suit, having returned earlier than expect from an away game, and he was standing in the kitchen making a list for a girl with quiet dreams and low expectations and who'd never had a real family.

Making her believe in him.

In them.

In those dreams.

"It's what he does," Mads whispered back. "He takes care of the people he loves."

"I—" Worry and panic and...hope.

No, hope was the most intense emotion in Vivi's eyes.

"It's what he does," Mads said again, squeezing her hand. "And it's what he needs to do." A beat. "Take care of *us*."

Teeth in a bottom lip.

Hope growing.

Then a breath, that chin coming up, and Mads watched this beautiful, generous, wounded girl take another step forward as she opened her mouth up and asked softly, "Do you think we can get some colored Sharpies too?"

Mads's heart squeezed when Lucas looked up from his list and smiled at Vivi. "Fine point or regular?"

"Fine—"

But he was already shaking his head and returning his attention back to the pad. "Both, of course. A writer definitely needs a shit-ton of Sharpies."

Vivi froze.

Then she giggled softly.

And it was the best sound in the world.

Thirty-Eight

Lucas

He was still wearing his suit, and his feet were protesting the dress shoes.

And he didn't give a fuck that his arms were full of heavy bags filled with shit he didn't recognize.

Rolls of sparkly tape that wasn't really used as tape.

Pens—at least he recognized those, but he didn't realize they'd come in the sheer breadth of colors and sizes and tip types (what the fuck?) that the stationery store had carried. And since he didn't know what Vivi would need and his girl wasn't the type to ask for anything (except Sharpies and fluorescent green cereal), he'd picked up one of each kind.

He could afford it.

And then she could figure out what type she liked.

Another bag held an organizer for all the pens, another a container for that strange tape and the notebooks and paper that were in a bag hanging from his other arm.

His trunk held a box with a new lamp and a desk that had made Vivi's eyes light up when she'd spied it in the furniture store that he'd pulled into after buying the haul at the stationery store.

Mads had gotten in on the action then, picking out curtains for Vivi's room and the lamp and baskets to organize her things.

And a chair that was tied on the rack on top of his SUV.

He needed to carry it in, put it and the desk together then head to the electronics store for a decent laptop.

First, though, he needed to carry these bags inside.

"You know, Mr. Playboy," Mads murmured, rising on tiptoe and pressing her lips to his jaw, "we can help too."

"Yeah," he told her. "By opening the door for me and helping Vivi sort all this shit into the hundred baskets you bought for her."

Mads's face gentled and her lips hit his jaw again. "Okay, honey."

She started for the front door since he couldn't fit his car in the garage with the chair on top, pulling her keys out of her purse as she went.

"Lucas?"

He turned, saw Vivi standing next to him, looking less uncertain and more...content or relaxed or...settled.

Like something had settled inside her over the last few hours.

"Yeah, sweetheart?"

She rocked back slightly on her heels then seemed to ground herself further. "Thanks for today."

"Anytime."

She studied him closely, mouth curving. "I never used to believe people when they said that. But you mean it." His heart thudded. "And so does Mads. And Ben and—" A shake of her head. "You just mean it."

"I do."

Silence. More studying.

More...settling.

"Can I carry something?" she asked after a moment.

His inclination was to demure. But he also sensed that she needed to help, needed to find her place.

So, he offered her up two of the lighter bags.

And they walked inside.

Settled. Hopeful.

And chock-full of writing supplies.

———

"I'll just take these boxes out, Peaches," he called, moving toward the open front door. "And then we can order pizza."

Thank God it was a Cheat Day.

"Sounds good, honey!" she called back.

He heard crinkling, knew she and Vivi were clearing up the trash, that they'd follow him out to the trashcans in a few with plenty of bags to cram inside.

He'd better get started on the cardboard.

At least he'd been able to change out of his suit.

His jeans and tee and boots were infinitely more comfortable. What *wasn't* was wrestling with the packaging, cutting and flattening it and playing Jenga in order to get it all to fit into the can.

"Here you go, honey," Mads said, her hair swept up into a ponytail, her cheeks flushed with exertion.

"I could have gotten it."

"I know." She kissed his cheek after he'd gotten it all thrown away and they started walking back across the front yard. "But I consider this my exercise."

"Picking out baskets and lugging trash bags?"

A shrug, eyes dancing. "Whatever works. Plus, one can say that shopping is the best type of workout."

He grinned, started to tease her back.

But then he heard it.

A familiar laugh—no a familiar *cackle*, and sweet Christ, he started to turn. Please tell him that he was hallucinating.

Or that he'd had a stroke amongst rolls of washi tape and this wasn't really happening.

But, nope, when he spun, he saw that his mom standing there —no, she was *wavering* there, probably so fucking high or smashed that it was a miracle she hadn't killed anyone on the way over.

Because, yup, her car was pulled up onto the curb, engine smoking, and, worse, his sisters were getting out of the back seat.

He'd heard a screech, a *thunk* as he'd been tossing the trash, but he'd assumed it Vivi or Mads with the bags.

Not his family showing up to shit on his peace.

"*Schlopping.*" Another cackle to punctuate the slurred words. "Exercise." His mom tossed her head back, laughed, and nearly ate shit before she managed to stagger a few paces left then right and stay upright. His head straightened, eyes locking with his. "That must be fucking nice."

"Inside," he said, nudging Mads to the front door.

"Who—" But she didn't finish the question because then she moved close and muttered. "Your family."

His breath felt like acid vapor in his lungs.

Burning, stealing his ability to speak.

Making him feel like that dirty little kid again.

"Police or Ben?" she asked softly, tight to his back, her gaze where his had gone before turning back to her at her question— away from his mom and sisters, who were all now clustered together, hanging over each other, and cackling as they wobbled their way up to him and Mads.

Ben.

Ben had come when their mom had pulled her shit, but Ben hadn't needed to do anything. Mads had found the strength within herself.

The strength to be something else.

"No," he whispered. "I just need..." A breath. "You."

And Vivi, but he wouldn't get his girl involved in what was sure to be a fucked-up messy scene, not when she'd been through far too much already.

Mads's body had stilled, but she recovered quickly, pressing herself closer to his back. "Fuck, I love you."

He loved her too.

So fucking much.

And he loved Vivi too, who'd sensed with those teenage abilities of hers—a teenager who had seen far too much for her years—that something was going down with her family and came out the front door.

"Lucas?" she called. "Mads?"

His sisters arrowed in on Vivi, their expressions turning nasty, leaning on their mom like a fucked-up *Hocus Pocus* trio.

Readying their venom.

Trying to drag him back into the past.

And...he didn't want to go.

He had his future right in front of him.

"Come on," he said softly, turning and wrapping an arm around Mads's waist, drawing her across the lawn, turning his back on the women.

On his past.

He walked up the stairs, bounded across the porch, slung an arm around Vivi's shoulders.

"Who're they?" she asked.

"Nobody important," he said, pitching his voice so his family could hear it. "Nobody who's a part of my life anymore. Nobody" —a glance over his shoulder, communicating a truth they probably wouldn't comprehend—"who will be part of my future. Because"—he turned back to the women who *were* his future— "I've got my future right here." A squeeze. "And they're fucking perfect."

Mads sniffed.

Vivi sniffed.

He chuckled, squeezing them one more time before releasing them and turning to shut and lock the front door.

"So," he said, forcing lightness. "Those are my mom and sisters."

"They..." Vivi bit her lip. "Don't seem *too* bad?"

No sooner had she finished the question then there was a crash on the porch and a thud and then pounding on the door.

And shouting.

Couldn't forget the shouting.

"I take my previous statement back."

He couldn't help it. None of this was the least bit amusing, but something about Vivi's wide eyes and her dry statement...

Well, somehow his girl had him laughing.

With his past literally banging on his door.

"You know what?"

Mads and Vivi both focused back on him.

"I think it's time for pizza."

Wide eyes.

And then they were both smiling.

"Yeah, honey," Mads murmured, moving toward him. "It's definitely time for pizza."

"Can we get garlic cheese bread too?"

He froze.

Mads's lips twitched.

His lips twitched.

And then all three of them were laughing.

And Lucas knew that he'd managed to shut the door on his past.

Without a huge confrontation. Without being dragged down into the depths of bad memories.

Instead with pizza, a woman at his back, and a girl who wanted to be a writer and had introduced him to the finer points of washi tape at his side.

Life was fucking perfect.

THIRTY-NINE

MADS

S he leaned back against the tree, twinkly lights overhead, blanket spread out beneath her, and was at peace.

Maybe she shouldn't have been after that scene with her mother weeks before and navigating through the complicated emotions in therapy and talking with Lucas afterward. Definitely she shouldn't be after seeing what kind of people Lucas had grown up with and the demons he'd had to fight to become the loving man she knew today.

But she was.

There were no more skeletons in their closets. She and Lucas were open and honest, their connection growing even though he was on the road half the time with the season fully underway. But they talked on the phone and texted and worked and spent time together when he was home. They made it work because they loved each other. And his love wasn't a noose. It freed her more and more every day, allowed her to be herself in safety.

Something Vivi was beginning to see she could do too.

She'd warmed after the scene with Mads's mother, more so

after Lucas's family had shown out of the blue and pulled their shit.

Plus, Nick had stayed gone, hopefully permanently because of the restraining order and Vivi out from beneath his thumb, and the fact that Pascal had begun to work to take him down.

All of which meant that Mads had seen her girl ease into her spot in the family she and Lucas were building.

Case in point, Vivi was here tonight.

Blowing off her friends to eat ice cream with Rome and Coop, chattering a million miles per hour as she stood next to them, her face lit up in a way that meant Mads would never regret hitting the gas so she could give Vivi a safe place to flourish.

She loved the girl in a way that made her heart feel like it was full of helium every time she saw her smile, saw her relax into her place with Mads and Lucas, with the guys and women and kids who'd opened their arms to her.

From hiding in the shadows to an important cog in the wheel of the Gold family.

Mads knew exactly how that felt—how scary and overwhelming...and *perfect*.

Vivi hadn't yet expressed scary or overwhelmed—at least not that Mads had seen. In fact, she'd slid right in, comfortable and blooming and instead of just small glimpses of the warm, funny girl, Mads and the others had that all the time.

It was great.

It was why she'd taken such a big leap in the first place.

Only, the more she thought about it, the luckier she felt. Because she wouldn't be here without that push to do something. And she wouldn't have been willing to take that leap without Lucas working his ass to prove to her that he saw her as someone different, someone lovable, someone worth buckling down and doing hard things for.

She was living in a fairy tale.

And her heart was fuller than she had ever thought possible.

Gold magic, she supposed.

Movement behind her, a soft, "It's me," from Lucas before he settled next to her, nudging her forward so he could slip between her and the tree, tugging her back against the strong, warm planes of his chest, wrapping his arms around her.

One warm palm hit her belly, sending it fluttering.

And those flutters increased when he held up a cup in front of her.

A smoothie.

She sighed.

He kissed the side of her neck and passed the cup over. "What's the matter, Peaches?"

"Nothing," she murmured, knowing even more deeply that she would have never allowed herself to be here, sitting on a blanket on the grassy expanse in front of The Dairy, stars and lights twinkling overhead, the air on the wrong side of cool for frozen treats, watching Vivi thrive, accepting her place in this big, expanded family, without the man who'd disappeared and then come back with the only dessert on the menu she liked. "It's just... my heart is happy."

His inhale was sharp and his hand flexed, drawing her even closer. "Mine is too, baby," he murmured, kissing the side of her neck again, holding her close even as they both fell silent.

Sitting and watching the happy chaos.

Until she remembered the drink in her hand.

She lifted the cup, took the straw between her lips, and drew up a sip.

Peaches.

Of course.

Her lips curved, and she was about to make a comment about different kinds of peaches—heh—when she heard, "Lucas!!"

Followed by pounding footsteps.

She turned, saw a little boy running toward them. He looked sort of familiar, like he'd been at one or two of the team events before, but she didn't know his name.

Or the name of the beautiful woman a few paces behind

him, striding after him in a hurried way that told Mads this was a common occurrence...and that the little boy didn't tire.

Ever.

Lucas started to shift and she rose with him, stepping to the side just as the little boy launched himself at Lucas.

Good thing her hockey player was strong.

He didn't miss a beat catching the little boy, sweeping him up into a hug. "Matteo! You made it."

A pouty bottom lip. "Mom said we can't stay too late since it's a school night."

"Well," Lucas said, ruffling his head before setting him back down on his feet and crouching so he was at eye level. "Your mom is right. It *is* a school night and because of that we're *all* heading out soon."

Matteo scowled.

"But we can get ice cream and play for a bit first," his mom said softly.

Mads glanced up from the sight of Lucas and the little boy, feeling something in her belly that she never thought she'd feel again.

Like maybe, someday, she might be ready for that.

Like maybe, someday, she would crave seeing Lucas kneeling in front of *their* kids.

Her heart gave one strong, hard pulse, and she had to look away.

"You cool if I take Matteo for a cone, Lauren?" Lucas asked, straightening and brushing his fingers against Mads's, silently asking her if she was okay with that too. Mads brushed his back, smiling up at him.

"Yeah, thanks," Lauren said, digging into her purse and pulling out her wallet.

"I got it," Lucas said, scooping Matteo up and settling him onto his shoulders.

"But—"

He ignored her, kissed Mads's forehead, and said, "Be back," already striding away as Matteo began to chatter.

"So, you're the one," Lauren said softly.

"What?" Mads asked, having to physically turn away from the sight that tugged on all of her heartstrings.

"I met him back before the season started, and I could see it on his face."

"See what on his face?"

Lauren was tucking her wallet back into her purse. "That you were the one for him."

Mads inhaled then exhaled and smiled when Lauren glanced back up. "In fairness, I think both of us were fighting it."

"Because he'd fucked up?"

This woman must have the freaking sight, but...there was also something about her that inspired Mads to confide. Maybe it was the kindness in her eyes.

Or maybe the sadness beneath it. Like she'd lost something precious.

"He did fuck up," she said softly. "But I did too. Plenty of times and that was hanging over both of our heads." She smiled. "It wasn't until the universe decided we needed a push before we were able to take a chance to move forward."

"And you're happy."

Not a question.

A statement.

Lauren smiled softly. "I like that."

"Me too," she murmured back, reaching over and squeezing Lauren's hand. Then because she wanted to see the bone-deep sad leave Lauren's eyes, she asked, "How did you meet Lucas?"

Lauren's expression warmed. "Where else with a hockey-crazed son?" She shook her head and chuckled. "At the rink. Lucas is Matteo's favorite player, and he was nice enough to take a few minutes with him, even though he was late."

Of course he had.

Because that was Lucas.

"And when he found out that Matteo's dad had passed away, he wouldn't take no for an answer when it came to including us."

Of course he had.

Accepting Vivi without blinking.

Making sure a little boy and his mom had a place.

Making sure that Mads never felt the sting of being on the outside, not ever again.

"Yeah," Lauren whispered. "That's what I saw on his face too."

Mads's lids flew open and she glanced over at Lauren, seeing the other woman's eyes were damp. She sniffed.

Lauren sniffed.

And then they both giggled.

"I never thought I'd be a romantic," Mads said to lighten the mood.

"With a hockey player like that in your heart"—she nodded to where Lucas and Matteo were heading back over, Matteo with an ice cream that was practically the size of his head—"how can you not be?"

She couldn't.

It was why she was all in on her hockey player.

FORTY

LUCAS

His woman had abandoned him, talking with Lily and a smiling Lauren, the two of them having somehow bonded in the five minutes that he'd been with Matteo getting the kid an ice cream.

Which had been devoured in approximately two minutes before Matteo had joined the flood of kids running around.

Kids with their dessert stomachs.

Lucas would be in a sugar coma right then if he'd tried to eat that much ice cream.

Grinning, he shook his head, started to turn away, intending to leave the girls to their chatting, knowing that the more connections they both made, the better. But as he started to rotate, his eyes caught on something that had him frowning.

Vivi was still with Rome and Coop.

Lily, Lauren, and Mads were a giggling trio.

But Pascal was there, standing in the shadows...and staring at the three women. No, staring at *Lauren*. Lucas frowned, feeling oddly protective, even though he was just starting to know her.

But Lauren had been through the wringer and while he liked Pascal, the other man was always there, always around, always quiet and lurking and what did they all really know about him except for the fact that he was good at security and always popping up like a groundhog—

Pascal's head swiveled, gaze coming to Lucas's.

He lifted a brow and then somehow melted into the shadows.

Right in front of Lucas's eyes.

He frowned into the shadows, started to move back toward his woman, patience at not holding her, not being with her, not having her body pressed to his and her scent in his nose waning. He wanted to take her home, wanted to soak in their time together since it was already in short supply with the season underway.

But the moment that he took a step toward Mads and the others, he saw Brit and Stefan.

They were almost in the shadows, maybe twenty feet from the spot where he'd sat with Mads earlier, and they weren't sneaking a kiss, taking advantage of a dark corner and quiet moment like more than a few of the other couples.

Their bodies were tense.

Their faces equally so.

And he couldn't hear the words they were exchanging, but they didn't appear to be the least bit affectionate.

Suddenly Brit reared back, hands falling to her sides, fisting.

Then her shoulders rose and fell on a breath, chin dropping toward her chest.

Stefan reached out as though he were going to touch her, but it was a moment too late. Brit was already turning away, already walking across the grass.

He watched the transformation come over her: the pain disappeared and her trademark smile locked into place. She joined a group of kids, sinking down onto the grass and helping her daughter, Roxie, open a container of bubbles, holding the wand up to Roxie's mouth so she could blow a stream of iridescent spheres.

They floated across the lawn, bobbing in the wind.

Then popped, one after another.

Fragile.

Delicate.

Gone.

He hoped that wasn't a sign.

But he didn't get the chance to think about that further. "Lucas!" Vivi called, and he glanced up to see her kicking a soccer ball in his direction.

He trapped it beneath his foot, kicked it back.

And it wasn't long before they had a gaggle of kiddos running up and joining in, Rome and Coop and him and Vivi all playing keep away as the littles chased after them like the tiny maniacs they were.

Before long, he wasn't thinking about Brit and Stefan, something he would come to regret later.

But by then Mads and Lauren had joined the game and Lily had jumped onto the kids' side, along with Mandy and Mia, and pretty soon it was a *game*.

Goals and sidelines being marked with baseball hats and purses.

People cheering from the makeshift sidelines—well, cheering for the kids' side and booing for him and Mads and the other adults.

It got competitive—or as competitive as the adults would allow because there were kids participating.

But shit-talk was happening—their fans showing no mercy to the adults.

And then, the rat, Vivi, switched sides, gathering the kids and Mandy and Mia together in a huddle that took several long minutes.

It broke up, and the kids unleashed a battle cry that told Lucas he and the other adults were in trouble.

T.R.O.U.B.L.E.

And then he experienced that *trouble* firsthand when Mandy chipped the ball to Mia, who passed it to Vivi. Vivi settled it and slid it to Matteo, who stopped it and then stood to the side, letting Roxie take it up the middle. The little girl dribbled like someone much older than her years, moving around the adults who were immobilized by a variety of collaborating kiddos who blocked and clung and generally made it so they couldn't save themselves.

Roxie carried the ball toward the goal...

And then across the goal line.

The crowd roared.

"Score!" Brit yelled. "That's my girl!"

Stefan was next to her, smiling, but his expression clouded when Brit moved onto the field, scooping up Roxie and pressing a kiss to her daughter's cheek.

He moved after them, and when he was within sight, Roxie extended her arms, silently asking for her dad, who took her against his chest, smiling when he ruffled her hair.

Something was very wrong with them.

But Lucas supposed all couples had their ups and downs.

He vowed to keep an eye on them both, though. Brit had spent the bulk of her time and energy making sure the guys and women of the Gold were happy.

And it seemed like...she wasn't.

If the expression on her face when Stefan walked off the field with Roxie in his arms, leaving her there amongst the others as he went and started packing up their stuff was any indication.

"What the fuck?" Rome muttered, and Lucas glanced over at his teammate, saw that Rome was taking in the same things he was. Brit pretending to be fine. Stefan walking away.

"I know," he muttered back.

But they didn't get the chance to talk further because the ice cream party was packing up.

The ball going away, the purses and hats that formed the goals and sidelines were retrieved and slung on shoulders, plunked on heads.

The kids were corralled by their parents and the trash picked up.

And everyone headed for their cars.

Including Roxie and Brit and Stefan.

FORTY-ONE

MADS

She was sweaty and exhausted.

From a soccer game played against children.

But, as usual, the Gold didn't do things in half measure, and the impromptu game had become a core memory.

Lucas slid an arm around her waist, tugged her against his side, leaning in and pulling...a leaf from her hair. He grinned, held it up in front of her.

She mock glared at him. "From you tackling me?"

"I was just breaking your fall."

"A fall you made happen," she said dryly.

"But I saved the goal."

Mads shook her head. Silly, silly man.

And so much freaking fun. Lucas, this night, this family of hers that was growing with beautiful, kind people while removing those who sought to drag her back.

All of it.

"Come on," she teased. "Let's get you home before you start trying to take Brit's spot."

He snorted. "Yeah, no. Couldn't pay me enough to stand there and get shot at."

"But you'll block pucks without all those fancy pads, so who's the smart one, huh?" she teased. Because it was true—he and the rest of the team would lay down and go full out to stop the pucks from getting to Brit in the first place.

Even if that meant putting their bodies between the puck and their 'tender.

A grin before he bent and kissed the top of her head. "Let's go get our stuff."

"Avoidance." She bumped her body against his. "Which means that you know I'm right."

"Oh, yup. Look! There's Vivi. And our blanket."

She started laughing, but it cut off when he tugged her to a stop, turned her around and cupped both of her cheeks. "What?" she whispered.

He bent, rested his forehead against hers. "Peaches."

"What?" she asked again, hands covering his.

"I love hearing you laugh."

Flutters. Always, this man was giving her flutters. "I love *you.*"

His face. God, the way he looked at her.

It was a dream, that fairy tale, and somehow it was her reality.

Pop!

She stiffened.

Pop! Pop! Pop!

"What's that—?" she began to ask.

But then some instinct deep inside recognized the sound for what it really was.

Gunshots.

And that was when the screams rang out.

"*Fuck!*" Lucas snapped, drawing her behind him as he whipped around, clearly searching for the source of the sound.

Pop! Pop! Pop!

Closer now.

Louder.

Lucas grabbed her hand and started to run, yanking her forward, dragging her along with him.

"Vivi," she mumbled. "Vivi!" she said louder, over the screams and commotion.

Over the pounding of her heart.

Lucas cursed again, running faster, and she realized he'd already been moving toward Vivi. Toward the girl—toward *their* girl.

She clutched his hand and together they sprinted toward Viv, who was no more than fifty feet away.

But they might as well have been on the other side of the Grand Canyon.

Because, out of the shadows...a familiar figure was emerging.

Tall, thin, with a rangy strength.

And holding a gun.

A gun Nick was lifting in Vivi's direction.

"Vivi!"

The voice wasn't Mads's, wasn't Lucas's.

It was Matteo's.

The little boy was sprinting toward Vivi, short legs pumping, expression determined as he clearly ran as fast as he could.

"Matteo!"

Lauren was running behind him.

But she was further behind, too far away.

Vivi screamed and Lucas let go of Mads's hand, ran even faster.

Because he'd seen Nick starting to turn, that gun beginning to point in Matteo's direction.

Fear clung to every cell in her body, but she didn't have time to freeze, to stop and watch in horror. Her people, her family...

It was shattering in front of her.

Lucas was close now, within five feet of Vivi and Nick and Matteo.

But he was too late.

Nick had turned, that gun had lifted, centered onto Matteo.

And Vivi's second scream just made him smile.

It was one that Mads had seen before, seen many times, one he gave right before he unleashed whatever sort of evil was in his head, the terror he got off on handing out.

Mads wasn't close enough to intervene.

Lucas wasn't going to get there in time.

But out of the shadows came Pascal, speeding forward, tackling Matteo...just as the gun went off again.

Loud, so fucking loud as the pair tumbled forward in a ball, rolling on the grass, crashing in a heap, Pascal's body wrapped protectively around Matteo's.

Nick froze, shock stealing that smile.

But only for a moment.

Lucas was within arm's reach...and suddenly had the gun pointed at the center of his chest.

Mads had felt terror, many times in her life, but she'd never known it to have a taste, to burn through each inch of her body, to steal every ounce of air in her lungs.

This was all-encompassing.

This was soul-stealing.

This was her fairy tale coming to an end.

"No!" she screamed, still running, knowing that she wasn't going to make it.

Nick looked at her.

Smiled that cruel, *cruel* smile.

Then he whipped the gun toward Vivi.

And fired.

Forty-Two

Lucas

He didn't know what made him react before the gun actually went off.

But he was moving before Nick spun toward Vivi.

Leaping at Vivi, shoving her back—

The gun went off and through the pain and ringing in his ears, he felt a hot slice of agony along his side.

Burning.

Cutting.

He shoved Vivi forward, knowing there wasn't time, knowing that Nick wasn't going to stop.

He'd seen it in the glint of the monster's eyes, in the smile just before he'd swiveled the gun toward Vivi.

"Run," he began. "Just run—"

The gun went off again and this time, the pain was more intense, exploding in his arm, radiating out in a way that made the edges of his vision start to haze.

He wavered, fell to his knees.

"Vivi, go!" he snapped.

"No!"

The scream came from behind him and had him whipping around.

He saw Mads running toward him.

He saw Pascal was up, having gotten Matteo and Lauren to safety, saw he was now running toward Mads.

But that wasn't what had Lucas's heart seizing, what had him struggling to get to his feet and finding that he couldn't get his legs beneath him—

No.

Oh, God.

What had panic seizing him, was that Mads was running toward that *monster*.

Who saw the movement...

And smiled.

That fucked-up, awful smile.

And squeezed the trigger.

FORTY-THREE

Mads

She saw his face.

Saw the barrel of the gun.

Saw the flash of it going off.

She braced for the pain...but it didn't come from where she expected.

A sharp shove had her falling forward, air squeezed out of her lungs, pain flaring in her ankle and radiating upward.

Pounding footsteps flew beyond her head and she watched Pascal tackle Nick, ripping the gun from his hands, shoving him face-first into the grass.

And then there were people streaming all around her.

Rome and Coop running in to help Pascal restrain Nick.

Mandy, with a bright red first aid kit, sprinting toward her, Blane on her heels. "Mads."

She was crawling toward Lucas.

Toward her hockey player.

Who wasn't moving.

She tried to get up, tried to stand, but her ankle wouldn't hold her. Mandy grabbed her shoulder, but Mads pushed her off. "Lucas," she rasped. "Get to Lucas."

Because he still wasn't moving, body on the grass, his arm extended in her direction.

Trying to get to her.

Trying—

A sob rose up in her throat as Mandy ran to kneel at his side, ripping open the first aid kit.

Mads kept crawling, inching closer, and then there was an arm under her. She gasped, glanced up, but it was just Rome, and he carried her to Lucas, setting her at his side before shifting around Mads's body and getting orders from Mandy, who slapped a bandage in his hand and ordered him to, "Put pressure there. Now."

She picked up Lucas's hand, tried to focus on his face and not the blood staining his clothes.

"Peaches."

Gasping, she looked up at his face, saw that his skin was pale, but his eyes were open.

"Lucas," she sobbed. "Oh, my God." Her throat felt like it was a second away from closing up completely. "Just stay with me," she forced out. "You're going to be okay. Mandy has you and—"

His fingers tightened around hers and he coughed, the sound awful and rasping and *not right*. "Peaches," he said again when he'd stopped.

"Yeah, honey." She smoothed her hand over his cheek. "Just breathe. I'm here. We're h-here. It's going to be okay."

He nodded slowly, eyes shutting for one long, slow blink that sent her heart convulsing.

"Stay awake," she ordered, squeezing her hand.

"You know"—he coughed and blood coated his lips, dribbled down his chin—"growing up with my family, I never thought I'd be able to really love a woman." He coughed again and the sound was horrible. "Never thought I could—" He coughed again, and

Mandy moved faster, shouting orders that Mads couldn't process, not when she was struggling so hard to hear Lucas's words.

She gripped his hand, leaned closer.

"I didn't think I would ever be good enough or open enough to make my own family," he pushed out.

"Honey," she said hoarsely, tears stinging her eyes, starting to drip down her cheeks.

"Then I got my head out of my ass and saw you. The real"— he coughed again, but it was weaker—"the real you and I knew that you would make all my dreams come true." He sucked in a rasping breath. "Even the ones I didn't know I had."

A sob caught in her throat, and she leaned in. "Lucas, honey, we'll make more dreams together, make more of them come true."

His lids slid closed.

She shook his hand, desperate to keep him awake. "But you have to stay here, have to stay with me and Vivi and—"

His arm went limp.

The fingers around hers loosened.

And her fairy tale ended.

FORTY-FOUR

LUCAS

"This is my fault," he heard distantly.

"Shh, honey," another voice whispered. "It's not your fault. It's not mine. It's Nick and him hating that we got out from under his thumb, hating that the police busted him because Pascal sent them enough evidence to break up his supply line."

He knew that voice.

Knew it so deep in his belly that he immediately began struggling through the layers of fog in his mind, trying to surface.

"But he—if I hadn't gone to live with you—"

"I used to date him, sweetie," Mads said. "If he'd wanted to find me, he could have at any time. Nick's just...evil and chose the moment that would hurt us all the most."

"I—"

Nick.

Nick.

The man who'd hurt Mads, who'd hurt Vivi, who'd come to the park with a gun and—

He managed to get his eyes open, to see his woman and his

girl sitting in hard plastic chairs, holding hands...and looking like hell warmed over.

"Lucas will be okay," Mads said softly, setting a crutch to the side as she leaned in and hugged Vivi. "The doctors said so, remember?"

Crutches.

His gaze slid down, saw the cast wrapped around Mads's leg from toes to knee.

"Peaches," he rasped, "what the fuck happened to your foot?"

Mads and Vivi froze, heads swiveling toward him.

Then they were moving, coming to his side.

Crying, touching him like he was fucking breakable instead of a big, tough hockey player and okay—he winced when Vivi's hug was just a smidgen too tight—maybe he was a bit breakable, at least right now.

The girl released him, and he saw the tears in her eyes, the way her throat worked.

"I love you, sweetheart," he whispered, lifting his arm with a herculean effort and cupping her cheek. Probably too much too soon but seeing Nick point that gun at her, the fear in his heart when she wouldn't leave even though he'd ordered her to go, meant that he wasn't delaying in sharing his feelings.

She was his as much as Mads was.

"I—" Those tears escaped and slid down her cheeks, and she face-planted on his chest.

Something that hurt like hell.

But he didn't nudge her back, just wrapped her in his arms and held her as she cried.

"Peaches," he said softly. "I'm okay."

"I know," she sobbed, lifting her head, her expression beyond gentle.

"What happened to your foot, baby?"

His question had the slightest bit of exasperation entering her eyes. "You had two gunshot wounds and nearly bled out, and you're asking about my foot?"

He just dropped his chin, held her eyes, and waited.

"I broke a bone in it when Pascal shoved me out of Nick's way."

His brows yanked together and she leaned a hip on his bed, probably taking weight off that broken bone.

And broken bone?

Pascal had broken her foot.

Seriously, the fucker was going to get a fist to the fucking face.

Mads touched his jaw. "Don't worry, Pascal's already beating himself up enough without any protective alpha tendencies making an appearance." She shook her head at his scowl. "Honey, look at me."

He *was* looking, studying every inch, seeing the scrapes on her forearms, searching for any other sign of injury.

"We're fine."

Searching for signs of injuries…and finding no other.

Because she was okay.

He was okay.

Vivi was okay.

"My girls," he croaked, touching Mads's hand, then Vivi's head. "You're okay."

Mads nodded. "And you are too."

He was.

They'd weathered a storm, made it through to the other side, and somehow, they were okay.

———

He sat in the booth, watching the guys on the ice below, hating that he wasn't out there with his team but thankful that he was *here*.

Out of the hospital.

Healing—more slowly than he would like.

Thankful that aside from his injuries and Mads's broken foot, no one else was hurt.

He'd started physical therapy today under the guidance of the team's doctors and those who'd taken care of him at the hospital.

It would be weeks before he got on the ice, longer before he actually played in a game again.

But he'd get there.

And it was worth every second of pain, frustration, and doctors' appointments in the meantime.

Because his girls were okay.

Because his family was okay.

The nightmares were still there—though he would never be more thankful than learning that Nick hadn't appeared until most of the guys had driven off, that all the young ones except for Matteo had been heading away from that fucking monster before he'd started shooting.

For those who'd remained at The Dairy, healing would take time.

But they'd get there.

Because they had each other.

Even now, he watched Lily, the team's sports psychologist, talking with Lauren. They both had eyes on Matteo and Vivi, who were putting together a puzzle before the game started.

The two had bonded before Nick's appearance on that once-peaceful night, and now they were even closer, leaning on each other despite the age gap. Lucas thought that Vivi needed some of Matteo's young resilience and innocence and Matteo couldn't go wrong with a surrogate big sister like Vivi.

"Hey, honey."

He glanced up at Mads, seeing the softness in her eyes.

He wound an arm around her middle, drew her down into his lap, grateful he could do that finally, that he was strong enough again and knew he wouldn't drop her if he did.

"Careful," she said, gently pushing against his hold, starting to stand up.

He touched her cheek. "The stuff of dreams, remember? We're making them happen."

Even if it was just holding his woman in his lap.

She sighed, gave into his hijacking of her body, and leaned her head against his shoulder. "You say the stuff of dreams," she murmured. "I say my fairy tale."

"Yeah, baby"—he stroked a hand through her hair—"it is a fairy tale."

She sighed again, this time in contentment he knew because she burrowed into him, murmured, "I love you," and settled against his body as he held her close, reminding her they were there and okay, sitting quietly while they watched his teammates below.

He could smell the dampness of the rink, feel the cool air on his cheeks, hear the cracks of sticks and the soft rumble of the crowd as the arena began to fill.

But he wasn't thinking about the past and all he'd missed out on because his parents were shit.

He wasn't thinking about all that Mads had suffered and how it was a miracle that she'd been able to push through and get to the other side.

He wasn't thinking about getting shot or how Nick could have devastated everything that he'd held dear.

This time the sounds of a rink were about a homecoming, about knowing he was finally in the right place and that he was surrounded by his family, his woman in his arms, the ever-present guilt finally gone, his future bright and within reach.

More to work toward.

More to achieve.

More to give the woman he loved, the teenager who had made a place for herself in his heart.

But happy, for once, with the life right in front of him.

Epilogue

Mads, Six Months Later

S pring was in the air, and her hockey player was about to start in his first game in six months.

More than half a season stolen by a man who'd just been sentenced to more than sixty-seven years in prison—for a collection of charges including assault, possession, intent to distribute, and money laundering. Oh, and attempted murder.

Nick would never invade their lives again.

Neither would her mother.

Who had shown up in the hospital with an apology on her tongue. Ben had sent her packing, same as he'd sent the vultures that masqueraded as Lucas's parents and siblings on their way. No exceptions. No more bullshit. No people who tore them down.

Just a family that supported and lifted each other up.

"Go, Lucas!" Matteo screamed, loud enough that Mads winced and rubbed at her ear, even with Lauren and the others a barrier between her and the little boy's enthusiastic cheers.

"Sorry," Lauren murmured from next to her. "He's a bit... excited."

Considering the way Matteo was bouncing in his seat, his

Clark-emblazoned jersey absolutely engulfing his little body, *excited* was a bit of an understatement.

She grinned at the other woman, who'd become a staple in their lives...and in the life of the man sitting on Lauren's other side.

Pascal.

That was a story for another day—as in, Mads hadn't gotten all the details yet.

But she would.

Because Lauren was family too.

"Let him be excited," Pascal said, no longer in the shadows, literally with the arena lights blazing, but also no longer in the dark when he wrapped his arm around Lauren, held her close and stared at the little boy who'd become his own as much as Vivi was Mads's and Lucas's.

Lauren smiled up at him, hand resting on his thigh, and pressed a kiss to his cheek. "Okay," she said softly and then turned back to the ice, her head on Pascal's shoulder, her expression one of a bone-deep contentment.

That, Mads recognized, because she had it too.

She exhaled as she stared out at the rink. They were sitting directly behind the players' bench, a spot she never would have chosen because they stood up half the time and blocked her view. But Lucas had said it was the only place that could fit them all, so she'd shut up, thanked him for making the arrangements, and was planning on hitting up the owner's box if she couldn't properly watch her man play.

For the moment, though, she was sitting between Lauren and the railing that overlooked the entrance leading to the bench at one end and back to the locker rooms on the other, watching the resurfacers finish, knowing that Lucas was soon going to be stepping out onto the ice. The crowd would go crazy. They'd been rooting for his recovery and comeback from the first moment it had been announced he would be okay. It seemed like the whole city was keeping one eye on his training, encouraging him to make it back.

It seemed like the whole city was watching tonight.

They weren't, of course, but a large subset was, and she knew by the determination on her man's face that he'd be playing his ass off that night.

He knew he was ready.

She knew it too, even if her insides were a giant ball of nerves.

The lights dimmed. A black carpet was rolled out onto the ice and the Gold's mascot appeared on the Jumbotron, setting the crowd off. They cheered loudly, knowing that Lucas was nearby, that one of their strongest players was ready to make his comeback.

Goldie, the glittering gold nugget costume which had been formerly manned by another of the Gold family, bounced a few times from her position just inside the door on the bench that the players entered the ice through before waddling out onto the carpet, a large black velvet bag in her hands.

Lucas hadn't mentioned that a ceremony was happening before the game, but she supposed it wasn't a surprise.

Of course the team would commemorate his first game back.

And...

There he was.

Her heart skipped a beat as he walked down the opening next to the railing, sending her a wink as he strode by. She watched as he bypassed the carpet, gliding onto the ice and raising his gloved hand in response to the cheers.

The center from the other team, Lake Jordan of the Sierra, entered from the other bench and moved to stand on the other side of the carpet.

Ceremonial puck drop.

Okay, that made sense.

But they usually had someone famous or from the community doing the actual—

"Mads."

She blinked, glanced down, and frowned.

Ben was standing in the opening that led to the players' bench, just on the other side of the railing.

In a suit.

As in, *not* in his hockey gear.

"What's the matter?" she whispered.

"Come here."

Brows drawing together, she glanced around. "*Here* where?"

"*Here*, here." He pointed at the black skate mat he was standing on.

Yeah, how was that going to happen?

She looked around again, but then Pascal was in front of her, crouching, mouth half-curved as he asked, "Need a lift?"

"I-uh—"

And then he was reaching for her hands, tugging her up out of her seat, and then—

"Eek!" she squeaked as he lifted her up and over the barrier and...

Into her brother's arms.

"What are you doing?" she whispered.

He cupped her cheeks, eyes blazing with emotion. "I am so fucking happy that I got my Maddy Girl back, you know that, right?"

His words sent her heart rolling in her chest. "Ben."

Then the heavy emotion faded and teasing entered the picture. "You know what I was most pissed about when I found out you got married in Vegas without me?"

She nibbled at her bottom lip, shook her head. "No, Benny."

"That I didn't get to walk you down the aisle."

Her throat seized, eyes immediately tearing up.

"So, I'm going to walk you down this one." He swiped his thumb beneath her eye. "No tears, Mads. This is a happy moment."

She fanned her face, hugged her brother, and then she let him link her arm through his and guide her forward.

Down an aisle lined with black carpet.

Toward a glittering gold nugget holding a large velvet bag.

Toward her hockey player, who was smiling at her like he had a secret—which, obviously, he did, considering she'd been plunked out of the stands and was now being led out onto the ice, spot lit beneath the gazes of twenty-plus thousand people.

Ben drew her to a stop, and then Lucas was holding her hand.

"What is this?" she asked.

He went down on one knee in answer.

She gasped, nearly fell over.

"Peaches, you deserve to stand in the light, for the world to see the brightness that shines through you each and every moment. And more than that"—he glanced over, accepted a folder from Goldie that must have been in that velvet bag—"you deserve to have a fairy tale wedding."

He opened the folder and she stared blankly at the papers.

Trying to comprehend the language.

Because it was a divorce decree.

"Trust me?" he said, holding up a pen.

It wasn't even in question. She took the pen, flipped to the marked page and signed.

"Mads." At her brother's voice, she turned, put the folder in Ben's outstretched hand.

And when she turned back, Lucas was holding a black box, a glimmering band of diamonds nestled in the velvet.

"Will you marry me?" he asked, still on one knee. "Again?"

The crowd had quieted, probably confused with all the folders and kneeling and signing.

But they understood a ring in a box.

And they understood her bursting into tears before leaping into his arms, causing them both to tumble to the ice. Lucas, no surprise, broke her fall, and then he was kissing her and the crowd was roaring.

And then Goldie was pulling other things out of her bag.

A veil that she stuck in Mads's hair.

A bouquet she shoved in Mads's hands.

A boutonniere she pinned to Lucas's jersey.

Bag empty, Goldie slid away, leaving Mads standing on the carpet, Lucas beside her, Ben close behind and...Lake Jordan in front of them.

He smirked, took the mic someone held out to him, and said...

"Dearly beloved, we are gathered here today..."

————

BRIT

Lucas's first game back had been a huge success.

But the impromptu wedding at center ice meant that the game hadn't started on time.

Which meant that it hadn't ended on time either.

And she'd still had to do her post-game routine, making sure she kept up with her conditioning, her strength training.

And, honestly, she didn't mind getting home late.

Roxie would already be asleep, so she wouldn't miss out on time with her daughter.

It would also mean less time in an empty bed, staring at the ceiling and trying to figure out how she'd managed to so thoroughly fuck up her life.

She hit the button to close the garage door, waiting until it shut completely before she unlocked the door into the house and stepped inside.

Pausing for her eyes to adjust to the darkness.

No under-cabinet lights left on for her in the kitchen, their soft glow illuminating her walk down the hall.

Not this season.

Maybe not ever again.

She sighed, hung up her coat, then toed off her shoes and shoved them into the rack before padding into the kitchen.

Dark.

Quiet.

She needed water, a snack, and then to sleep so she'd be rested enough to get up with her rambunctious kiddo.

Stretching, she hit the switch for those under-cabinet lights.

Then gasped, clamping a hand to her throat.

Stefan was sitting on one of their stools. Silent. Staring at her. And having sat in the dark for who knew how long.

"Hey," she managed past her pounding pulse, her suddenly tight throat.

Where had the warmth in his eyes gone?

Had it just disappeared one day?

Or had it slowly, incrementally just faded away, slipping from his blue irises like grains of sand in an hourglass, so slowly that she hadn't noticed?

Not until they were empty.

He didn't reply, and since she didn't know what to say to this man who'd become a stranger by millimeters, she turned for the fridge.

She'd cut up some veggies, dip them into some hummus, drink some chocolate milk, some water, and call that a good enough recovery meal.

After grabbing a pack of carrots and celery, a pepper, some kale, she spun back around.

Set them on the counter.

Snagged a cutting board, a knife.

Was about to start slicing when her husband finally spoke in a tone that had become familiar over the last year.

Cold.

Sharp.

Resolute.

"I want a divorce."

———

Rome

I glanced at my phone screen in disbelief.

Because I couldn't possibly be reading what I was reading.

I couldn't possibly be getting this news through social media and not through a phone call or an in-person meeting or—

My cell rang, blocking out the news story on the screen that someone had tagged me in.

And the number had my stomach clenching.

My agent.

I swiped, lifted it to my ear. "Devon, hey."

Silence that had my stomach going from clenching to churning.

"Rome, hey, buddy."

Fuck.

I knew that tone.

I knew that I wasn't going to like this news.

"Just tell me, Dev," I said, pushing up off my couch, striding across the room, too antsy to stand still. Ants were crawling under my skin, my nerves were jumping, making my muscles tense. I felt like I'd been doused in lighter fluid and was one second away from someone tossing a lit match onto my body and setting me on fucking fire.

"Well..."

I crouched, free hand in my hair, bracing for the hit I knew was coming.

And then it did.

"Rome, buddy," Devon said. "It's not good news."

No shit.

But I didn't say that, just waited, crouching there in my living room, TV blaring in the background, fingers gripping my hair so tightly that I wondered distantly if I was at risk of tearing it from my scalp.

Didn't say anything as I waited for Devon to drop the rest of the bomb.

And drop it he did.

"You've been traded to the Eagles."

———

Thank you for reading! I hope you loved Mads and Lucas as much as I did! The next book in the Gold Hockey series is SCORED. **Find out if Brit and Stefan can navigate their way to a happy ending a second time...or if time and life and *hockey* has driven them apart for good.**

CLICK HERE TO GET SCORED NOW>

———

What's going to happen when Rome has to face off against the team that's become his family?
Check out the first book in my brand new Eagle Hockey series, BROKEN LACES! This team of misfits and bad boys are going to puck you in the best possible way!

CLICK HERE TO PREORDER BROKEN LACES NOW>

———

Want to know what happened between Lauren and Pascal?
GOLDEN—their story—is going to be available exclusively via my Kickstarter coming next month!

CLICK HERE TO GET NOTIFIED ON LAUNCH>

Are you ready to meet Lake Jordan, star forward for the Sierra, underwear model, and the man everyone hates to play against? Lake's book, OVER THE LINE, is coming this November!

CLICK HERE TO GET OVER THE LINE NOW>

If you enjoy my series, considering supporting me on PATREON! Get access to early releases, bonus content, character art, audiobooks, special edition covers, swag, and much more!

CLICK HERE TO SUPPORT ME>

———

Hate missing Elise's new releases? Love contests, exclusive excerpts and giveaways?

Then signup for Elise's newsletter here!

www.elisefaber.com/newsletter

———

And join Elise's fan group, the Fabinators (https://www.facebook.com/groups/fabinators) for insider information, sneak peaks at new releases, and fun freebies! Hope to see you there!

———

I so appreciate your help in spreading the word about my books, including sharing with friends! Please leave a review on your favorite book site!

GOLD HOCKEY SERIES

Also by Elise Faber

Coasting

Centered

Charging

Caged

Crashed

A Gold Christmas

Cycled

Caught

Cap

Covered

Crushed

Changed

Scored

Breakers Hockey (all stand alone)

<u>Broken</u>

<u>Boldly</u>

<u>Breathless</u>

<u>Ballsy</u>

<u>Bewitched</u>

Blowout

Breathe

Blazed

Sierra Hockey Series

Over the Line

The Big Skate

Caught from Behind

On the Fly

Rush Hockey Trilogy #1

Big Puck Energy

Filthy Puckboy

So Pucking Over It

Rush Hockey Trilogy #2

Love, Pucks, and Other Stories

All's Fair in Pucks and War

No Pucks Lost Between Us

Eagles Hockey Series (all stand alone)

Broken Laces

Love, Action, Camera (all stand alone)

Dotted Line

Action Shot

Close-Up

End Scene

Meet Cute

Love After Midnight **(all stand alone)**

Rum And Notes

Virgin Daiquiri

On The Rocks

Sex On The Seats

Life Sucks Series **(all stand alone)**

Train Wreck

Hot Mess

Dumpster Fire

Clusterf*@k

FUBAR

Perfect Storm

Free Fall

Lost Cause

Roosevelt Ranch Series (all stand alone, series complete)

Disaster at Roosevelt Ranch

Heartbreak at Roosevelt Ranch

Collision at Roosevelt Ranch

Regret at Roosevelt Ranch

Desire at Roosevelt Ranch

Phoenix Series (read in order)

Phoenix Rising

Dark Phoenix

Phoenix Freed

Phoenix: LexTal Chronicles (rereleasing soon, stand alone, Phoenix world)

From Ashes

In Flames

To Smoke

KTS Series (all stand alone, series complete)

Riding The Edge

Crossing The Line

Leveling The Field

Scorching The Earth

Cocky Heroes World

Tattooed Troublemaker

About the Author

USA Today bestselling author, Elise Faber, loves chocolate, Star Wars, Harry Potter, and hockey (the order depending on the day and how well her team -- the Sharks! -- are playing). She and her husband also play as much hockey as they can squeeze into their schedules, so much so that their typical date night is spent on the ice. Elise is the mom to two exuberant boys and lives in Northern California. Connect with her in her Facebook group, the Fabinators or find more information about her books at www.elise-faber.com.

facebook.com/elisefaberauthor

amazon.com/author/elisefaber

bookbub.com/profile/elise-faber

instagram.com/elisefaber

tiktok.com/@elisefaberauthor

goodreads.com/elisefaber

www.ingramcontent.com/pod-product-compliance
Lightning Source LLC
Chambersburg PA
CBHW071554110726
47908CB00007B/2094